CONTENTS

HIS SECOND CHOICE	5
Chapter 1	6
Chapter 2	21
Chapter 3	30
Chapter 4	42
Chapter 5	66
Chapter 6	75
Chapter 7	84
Chapter 8	89
Chapter 9	101
Chapter 10	126
Chapter 11	133
Chapter 12	147
Chapter 13	154
Chapter 14	172
Chapter 15	184
Chapter 16	194

Chapter 17	199
Chapter 18	207

For: Chloe, Charlotte and the countless young souls looking for love........

" If I could tell you one thing, it'd be this. Never settle. Don't settle until you get what you deserve and it is everything you have ever desired. Wait for the person who you can tell them everything about you, past, present future, and they won't doubt your spirit. Wait for the person you can trust entirely, who makes you want to be a better person, but certainly makes you happy that you are you. Wait for the person who makes you feel so alive, brings out the best in you and makes you smile, just as you would for them. You wait for your person, and never dare to settle for less."

HIS SECOND CHOICE

By: Lisa Doherty

CHAPTER 1

The first week of September was always bittersweet for Halyn Curtis. The freedom that came with the summer break had ended, and it was the beginning of another school year. Although she enjoyed school and learning in general, she knew exams, projects, and volunteer service hours were going to creep up on her quickly. However, this year was far more momentous as it was the start of a new chapter, a new era of sorts. At nineteen, she was now a first year college student.

She slammed down on the snooze button to the notoriously annoying sound of her alarm clock. As she lay on her back, she could feel the sweat under her long brown hair, against her neck. "I must have been dreaming." She thought to herself. She further awoke to the sound of the rain slapping forcefully against her dorm room window, with the muffled echo of her roommate humming an off-key tune in the shower. As she was about to roll over and catch another few precious moments of sleep, Rowan, her twin sister began to violently knock at her door. Rowan was already dressed for class, makeup fully applied and hair perfectly placed in a sleek high ponytail. Halyn always wondered how her sister had so much energy at the crack of dawn each and every morning. As kids, Rowan was always the first to be awake in the house, and this transcended into adulthood. On the weekends, she would often go to the gym, be showered, and had her morning coffee all before Halyn had even opened her eyes. Her natural beauty and lack of time it took her to look attractive was something Halyn had always envied about her sister. Rowan's hair had a natural auburn sheen, her facial features were perfectly symmetrical, and her dainty yet bouncy walk made even the most crotchety people smile. She exuded confidence, something Halyn was always envious of.

"Hey, get up! How are you still in bed? Anatomy 101 with the hot Professor starts in an hour." Rowan wasn't trying to hide her excitement. She was recently single, so if there was a decent looking male around, she was there to impress, fake eyelashes batting and all.

"I'm getting up now. I'm just waiting for Ellie to get out of the shower."

"How is she?" Rowan asked as she barged in through the doorway, jumping into Halyn's bed.

"She's alright. I haven't had the chance to get to know her. She keeps to herself mostly and talks to her boyfriend until two in the morning every night. Between her late-night, long-distance love conundrums, and the five a.m. post-club heard of elephants in the halls, I'm on thin ice to how nice of a human I will be today. Thank goodness for earplugs and white noise apps".

"Well, that's college for you. You ought to get used to it. Straight A's are going to be harder to achieve in this place. Now get up, I think Barbara Streisand has called it quits in the shower. I'll wait for you at the café. Vanilla latte?"

"Yes, please. I'm going to need it" Halyn replied thankfully.

It had only been a few days since Halyn had arrived at Dryden College and she knew that it was going to take some adjusting. She had always lived in the same city, on the same suburb street, and in the same house for most of her childhood. She grew up in a small city, and it was nothing special, but still, it was home for her and that meant that even the biggest, brightest and busiest cities were going to be out of her comfort zone.

Dryden College was located in Harlowe, a city in Canada, just north of the border that was known for its contemporary fashion and it was overrun by the privileged. You didn't live there unless you had money, or inherited money, or worked with a lot of money. And although Halyn did not have the worst upbringing, she certainly had no clue how to fit into such a society. Halyn had always held up part-time jobs to get by. She had to pay for the majority of her schooling with her savings but balanced it with enjoying some of the finer things in life, like lattes. She was from a working family. Her mother always made sure she and Rowan were her priority. Her parents were shy, didn't have a large social circle, and kept to themselves, a far cry from her highly extroverted sister. To Halyn, it was perplexing how different each person in a family could be and even more so, how strikingly different twins could be. Halyn and Rowan grew up in the same home, the same environment, with the same friends, and they were polar opposites in many ways, but still managed to somehow be each other's closest companion.

Halyn turned on her music and slid into the shower quietly, just in case the other students in the room next to her were sleeping. The warm, crisp water against her face and the smell of fresh lavender soap were exactly what she needed on this cool, rainy day. But, she needed that vanilla latte to function, so she quickly finished her shower. As she reached for her robe, she thought about how she was going to balance friends, family, schoolwork, along with the pressures to fit into this new intimidating environment. She had been successful in balancing her life until this point, but she needed to do well in college. Although she achieved high grades throughout high school, it never came easily. This always annoyed her. There was always someone in class that she envied for achieving a ninety percent average, even though they never showed up. Delicately, Halyn slipped into her favourite pair of skinny jeans and brand new blush pink wrap sweater. She threw her long, freshly clean hair up in a low bun, grabbed an umbrella, and headed downstairs.

Rowan was sitting at the table by the door, eyeing up the tall, lean and sheepish barista. "He's cute! Look at those eyes. " She whispered.
"They're green." Halyn sarcastically replied. Rowan looked at her sister with a fierce glare.
"If eyes could kill. Why don't you go ask him for his number? Don't ask him to go for coffee though because he does work in a coffee shop".

Rowan took her desperate look off the broad-shouldered man when he met her gaze. He smirked and wiped his hands on his tight-fitting apron. "He could probably get the coffee for free though. Anyway, he's not my type. I was thinking he may be yours though".

"You know I'm not looking right now. It's only been three months since Chase and I broke up and trust me, I'm not ready". Halyn stated as she took an aggressive sip of her coffee.

"You were too good for him anyway. He was lazy and you enabled it. It was never going to work." Sometimes Rowan's matter of fact, condescending approach to important conversations annoyed Halyn, but she knew it was never worth the fight to oppose anything she said. Rowan's perception was her reality and Halyn would manage just fine by biting her tongue. Plus, sometimes she was the voice of reason and was just the person she needed to bring her back to reality.

They walked to their first class briskly, taking in the enthusiasm of the other students they passed. Rowan's jaw dropped at the sight of their Professor, who came bounding down the concrete staircase. His name was Charles and he was married, but somehow, Halyn didn't think that would stop her sister from showing interest in him. Not that she thought of her as a homewrecker, but that it wouldn't stop her from flirting a little and putting an apple on his desk now and then. However, she had to agree with Rowan, he was not hard on the eyes. He fit in well with the typical urban city crowd at Dryden. His salmon-coloured suit jacket over a paisley dress shirt and skinny dark jeans were fashion-forward and even Rowan, the fashionista, was impressed. It was determined by both sisters, that he would become a quick favourite to the students.

"Good morning class. Today is day one of Anatomy 101 and that's right, it is.....quiz day."

"Quiz Day?" Halyn thought. "How could there be a quiz on the first day of classes?" Even though she absorbed most of her anatomy lectures from high school, she didn't care for the surprise quiz. Professor Charles was already turning her hair gray.

After the quiz, she sat back and studied the

room. The silence was intimidating and almost every student had their faces glued to their notes. She determined there was going to be some stiff competition in the room. Halyn was a people watcher and she had an intuitive radar on personality types. There were many students she felt she could relate to in the class, which was relieving. No one stood out to her until the door at the back of the class opened. A new student walked to the back of the room, making a scene with her loud high heels and rustling her belongings, in hopes that everyone would notice. Halyn's eyes widened. She recognized the attention seeker immediately. It was an old friend from primary school, someone that she knew well, but they had drifted apart in high school. Her name was Marissa Jacobs. She was the envy of all the girls growing up. This was probably because she had a perfect physique and dressed in designer fashion from head to toe, which was all people seemed to care about nowadays. Dryden was a magnet for the wealthy, and it came as no surprise to Halyn to see her on campus, but it was perplexing to see her in this particular classroom. The boys loved her and it seemed as though they still did because the testosterone seemed to peak when she flawlessly took her seat. She was statuesque and had gorgeous long red hair. Marissa reluctantly caught Halyn's gaze and smirked out of the corner of her delicate perfectly dimpled mouth. Halyn smiled back and at that same moment, she felt Rowan's elbow dig into her ribs.

"Is that Marissa Jacobs?" she asked angrily.
"Yes, yes it is."
"She's so ugly," Rowan said sarcastically.
"You're so superficial," Halyn replied.
"What is she doing here? I thought she was sailing on her parent's yacht for the year?'
"Beats me, I haven't talked to her in a long time."

Finally, after 3 tedious hours of anatomy, the class was let out. As Halyn was ready to walk out the door, she felt a pull on her arm. " Oh hi Haley! Marissa's voice rose three octaves as she greeted her unwanted classmate.

"It's Halyn. And you know that"
"Of course it is. It has been such a long time since we were friends, it must have slipped my mind."

Halyn swallowed her pride, put on a big smile, and killed her with kindness. "Hi, Marissa. It's nice to see you. Did you just join the Health Sciences/Pre Med program today?"
" Yes, I just transferred from Political Science. Not for me. I'm going to be a doctor!"
" Still as overconfident as ever," Rowan snapped back.

Halyn refrained from mentioning that she also had plans to become a doctor, a pediatrician to be exact. She loved children and always thought she would have four of her own. But, she also knew that many of the other students in her current class, Anatomy 101, had similar plans for their future. It was competitive and cut-throat at Dryden. She hoped her grades and volunteer experience and would be enough to get in, but she had four hard years ahead of her.

"Well, it was nice to see you. I'm sure we will be seeing a lot of each other." Halyn forced out a second smile. Something about this tedious conversation with Marissa still didn't sit right with her. Even though she hadn't seen Marissa in years, and kept reminding herself that they were no longer in high school, something told her she was the same spoiled and complacent girl she always was growing up. Halyn remembered the rumours Marissa had started about her classmates and also how many boyfriends she nonchalantly stole from other girls in her grade. Halyn felt free and content with the dissociation from Marissa and she had no plans to let her back into her life, other than the odd group project, and maybe running into her at the cafe.

Halyn casually made her way to the washroom so that she didn't have to endure any more small talk. She needed some time alone to absorb the latest anatomy lesson. Her plan failed when she was stopped in the hallway by Rowan who was holding a bright yellow flyer in her hands. It read:

FIRST YEAR FLING- BLACK AND WHITE BALL
Grand Hall – Dryden College
All first-year students welcome!
Friday, September 19th
8 PM

" We need to go to this ball!" Rowan insisted "It sounds fun, and we could both use a night out."

Halyn hesitated at first but then realized she hadn't participated in any orientation activities, and she needed to meet her new classmates. Her parents reminded her daily throughout the summer that her college years would be the best years of her life and that it was where she would make lifelong friends. " I hope they are right." she thought to herself.

"Ok, I'll come. But let's keep it tame. I don't want you leaving me there on my own while you ditch me for some guy like last time."

" I wouldn't do that to you here. What kind of sister do you think I am? But I'm also not bailing at 9 PM because you want to study the next day. It is our first year, after all, it's our time to shine!"

" Well, that sounds reassuring," Halyn replied sarcastically. Rowan turned away, clicking down the hall in her four-inch red leather heels.

Halyn sighed loudly. Rowan's reaction

meant that it was not going to be a tame night. Her sister was known for being a socialite. She knew of all the best parties, events, and places to be on any given weekend. She was always the life of the party too. Halyn enjoyed most outings with her, but she cherished her sleep. Furthermore, making sure they flagged a cab home was more important than being one of the cool kids.

Later that night, Halyn sat in her dorm room deciding how to decorate it so that it provided a relaxing, tranquil atmosphere that was perfect for studying. She couldn't help but notice how quiet it was for a Friday. Other than the muffled sound of Ellie's nauseating conversation with her boyfriend in the background, it was quite peaceful. She made herself a cup of calming lavender tea and opened her biology textbook. She started to study when she got a text message from Chase. Ignoring it, she rolled her eyes and kept reading her book, but she wasn't able to concentrate. Why was he messaging her again? He wasn't over their relationship. She opened the pop-up screen regretfully and read the message with as little animosity as possible.

"I hear Marissa is joining the Health Sciences class at Dryden. Is this true?"

Halyn leaned back in her office chair and took some time before she replied. After all, she knew he was just trying to push her buttons, and strike some sort of conversation to grasp her attention, so little words would go a long way.

"Yes. Why?"

"I'll have to tell the guys she's there. Is she single?"

"I don't know Chase. She's not my friend, and besides, it's day one. Don't you have someone else who can help you with your matchmaker queries?"

" No one else that I care to talk to. I'll let the guys know though".

"Bye Chase."

    Chase had turned into the kind of person Halyn couldn't tolerate. He was arrogant but had no reason to be. He was the local jock from high school who proceeded to do nothing with his life, chasing after fading dreams of becoming a pro, but he still thought he was above everyone else. Their relationship was always one-sided and centered around his needs, friends, and extra-curricular activities and she soon came to learn that Chase and his friends were respected for their talent in basketball, but not well-liked as people. Halyn looked at the bright red numbers on her clock. She gasped when she read 1:07 AM. She couldn't believe she had been awake for so long studying.

    After getting into her flannel pyjamas and settling into her soft down-filled bed, Halyn couldn't help but think about why people were so enamoured with Marissa Jacobs. In high-school, it made sense because she was the first to develop breasts and a body like a model. Her outgoing and overconfident personality seemed to spread like osmosis anywhere she went, as she effortlessly commanded a room. As much as Halyn was confident with who she was and what she had achieved so far, she still felt a pang of jealousy towards Marissa. With that thought, Halyn soon drifted to sleep.

The next morning, Halyn woke up early to fit the gym in after studying. The gym was located in the same building as the library, so she packed up both her book bag and gym bag and headed for the Central Hub, on the main campus. The trees were turning into a cornucopia of colors, with leaves falling softly to the ground. Halyn delighted in the sound of them crunching under her boots, and this was the first sign that fall was around the corner.

The library was spacious and luxurious, far grander than any other library she had ever stepped foot in. It was eleven stories high and it housed many sections designated for specific student groups, including separate floors for international students and post-graduate students. It had a trendy café on the first floor and rooms with the most comfortable plush lounge chairs and beanbag beds. The crackling of the fireplaces on each floor set the mood for the perfect studying atmosphere, a sort of haven for Halyn. She could see how this would become her favourite place to both study and relax, as she pictured herself there on a crisp winter day with a warm beverage in hand, cozied up by the fire. Halyn found a booth with a long wooden table directly beside a window where she could see the pristine waters of the lake in the distance. It was the perfect place to shut the world out. She placed her bags beside her and opened her anatomy textbook. She had only read one chapter before she noticed a shadow peer from behind her seat. She turned around to see Marissa standing over her, with a smile fit for a woman who had just murdered her husband for his money.

"Hi Halyn, are you going to class in the morning? I was hoping I could get a ride?"

Halyn begrudgingly smiled back. She wanted to say no but couldn't come up with even the lamest of excuses. " Say no Halyn, say no," she repeated in her mind. "Sure. Which residence are you in?"

"Oh, I live off-campus." Daddy bought me a place just down the street on Seaside Rd. I couldn't possibly live in the dungeons they have here."

It was so Marissa of her to say something so disrespectful. Marissa Jacobs came from money, and not just some money, lots of money. Her Grandparents started a movie theatre chain and her parents inherited most of the money once her Grandparents passed away. No one knows if Marissa even knew her extended family. Let's just say she was neither modest nor humble about her inheritance. She knew how to flaunt her wealth and used it to her advantage. Having never worked for anything in her life, she expected everything to be handed to her without ever showing any gratitude, and yet, here she was saying she was going to be a doctor. In her mind, her parents would just simply pay her way in, taking a spot in medical school from someone who deserved it."

"Do you not have a car?" Halyn asked.

"It's not here yet. They sent the car in the wrong damn color last week. There is no way I'm driving a boring beige sedan around this city. I get my silver Benz SUV next Thursday."

Halyn rolled her eyes in her mind. "I'll be there at 8 a.m." Halyn replied regretfully. She dreaded tomorrow morning already.

CHAPTER 2

Zach Payne learned how to build his own car. He worked day in and day out all summer to put together the smallest little engine that could. It wasn't the most upscale car on the street, but it got him from point A to point B. Even though his father could have bought him his own luxury vehicle to show off, he was proud of what he had accomplished and his parents made him earn the things he wanted. Nothing was given to him for free. The forced independence made Zach a bit annoyed at times, but as his parents always re-enforced, it would make him more responsible in the end. He climbed into his rickety car and adjusted his mirrors. The cold leather seats startled him as his roommate Eric stepped into the passenger side.

"Why are we driving two blocks again?" Eric asked.

"Because I need to test the brakes. I thought I heard something yesterday. I think they may be a little off."

" Oh, thanks man, glad I could be your crash test

dummy." Eric voiced sarcastically.

Zach and Eric had been close friends for as long as they could remember. They went to summer camp as kids and as any other thirteen-year-old boys would do, they spent many summer nights pulling pranks on the girls in the bunks by the lake. Zach loved going to summer camp because it allowed him to get away from the dysfunctional chaos of his home life. He felt the same way about going off to college. He no longer had to listen to his disgruntled father criticize him about his lack of athletic ability. Nor did he have to listen to the constant bickering from his mother about how his father worked too much and was never around when he was a child. He always thought they should have divorced a decade before they finally called it quits. For many years, he told himself that he would find the woman of his dreams after living a lavish bachelor lifestyle for a while. He had no plans to settle down anytime soon and in the back of his mind, he felt that blaming his parents was the best way to deal with his commitment issues. He planned to simply enjoy his college years, single, and without being tied down in a relationship.

" So, now that you are single again, what do you say we scope out all of the eye candy today?" Eric suggested eagerly.

" I guess there is no harm in that, but not today. I'm kind of focused on the car and actually paying attention in class."

"Come on man, this is college. These are going to be the best years of our lives."

"I know, but I prefer not to look for it you know? When I find the right girl, it will happen when it is supposed to. But right now, I'm not looking for anything."

" What's wrong with you? It's like you just walked out of one of those cheesy made for TV movies. This isn't the Zach I know. The Zach I know would be rating all the girls on a scale of one to ten during our first class."

"Maybe I'm maturing." Eric and Zach both let out an honest laugh.

As he daydreamed about his anticipated bachelor lifestyle, Zach felt a jerk under his right foot. Then it happened again. After a series of jolts under the front of the car, he realized that the gas pedal was stuck. In an anxious fury, he tried to pull up on the pedal and down on the brakes, sweating and kicking until the car finally slid rapidly to an abrupt stop at a busy intersection. It all happened within a matter of moments, but it felt like an eternity. He rested his head on the steering wheel, in less of a panic, trying to catch his breath. Out of the corner of his eye, he saw a slender, rather mousy, yet attractive girl standing two feet from the front bumper of the car. Realizing what he had done, he removed his head from the steering wheel and flung the driver side door open, and as it started to come off its hinges, he desperately started apologizing to her. "I'm so sorry. The gas pedal was stuck and I tried to.........."

Halyn Curtis proceeded to hit the front end of his broken-down car and kept walking forward assuredly, keeping her anger in check. Zach was mortified. " I need to get the brakes and pedals fixed stat! I'm almost running over people for goodness sake." He felt terrible for the girl he almost hit and turned the corner to try and follow her so he could apologize to her face to face, but she was gone.

" What a moron. I can't believe he almost hit you!" Shouted Rowan. What if he actually hit you? That would be a great way to start the first week of school. Was he on his phone? Was his music really loud?"

"Calm down Rowan. I'm the one who almost got hit remember? He just seemed like he was out in left-field like he had something on his mind. And I realize that the outcome could have been worse, but let's drop it and move on."

They walked into the bustling classroom and sat down in the second row. Rowan wanted to make sure that Professor Charles could see her well. She had put on her best outfit for the occasion. The night before, she had envisioned throwing him a few subtle glances here and there, in hopes that he would find her at the very least intriguing and sexy. She craved the attention.

" I thought you were supposed to pick Marissa up with Ellie's car this morning."

"I was." Replied Halyn. She had a frustrated tone to her voice and it quickly became apparent to Rowan that Halyn had gone to pick her up and Marissa wasn't there.

"She wasn't there was she?"

" No, no she wasn't." Halyn sighed as she removed her multi-colored pens from her book bag.

"Where was she? Eat too much caviar last night? Or did she hire a limo for the day?"

Halyn turned around and noticed that Marissa wasn't in class after all. She had never met anyone so inconsiderate in her life. "I have no idea. All I know is that I'm not agreeing to pick her up again any time soon."

From three rows behind, out of the corner of his eye, Zach saw the girl he had almost run over on his way to school. He felt a sudden flood of panic in his chest, and Eric saw it in his face. "Dude, your face is redder than the stop sign you almost blew this morning." Eric looked in the direction of Zach's gaze. Oh hey, it's the girl you almost crushed!"

"Honestly, could you please be a little louder next time? I don't think the staff in the lunchroom heard you. And yes, I should go apologize to her."

"No man, just play it cool. She won't recognize you anyway."

"I'm really that memorable am I?" Zach was

slightly insulted but didn't feel the need to listen to Eric. He felt bad for the girl and he knew that at some point she would see him drive his car into the parking lot. He squeezed past the other students in her row and tapped her on the shoulder. Halyn turned around and immediately scowled.

" Can I help you?" She asked

" Hi. I'm Zach Payne. I'm incredibly sorry that I almost hit you this morning. I truly am. You see, I've been building the car myself and I was testing it out and…….." He looked to his left, and leaned back reactively, dodging an attack. Rowan's pupils grew three sizes as she leaned towards Zach, about to rip a hole in his face. Halyn stopped her in her tracks.

"It's ok. I have this one Rowan," her confidence fading with every passing second. She gave him a tolerant smile that belied the irritation she felt inside. " Well Zach, I appreciate the apology, but you really should pay attention when you are driving from now on. I could have been an old lady or a child."

" That's very altruistic of you to think that," he said

" Oh, a man of big words I see. Well, thanks for the compliment, but I'm trying to recover from almost dying this morning, so if you would please excuse me, I'd like to get back to focusing on my work."

Professor Charles bounded through the

doors of the classroom, attempting to balance his pile of books and paper as he began to lecture before he even made it to the front of the room. He barely had his coat off before he was drawing heart chambers on the blackboard. Flustered, all of the students in the room began to rustle their notebooks and started copying his notes.

" Well, I guess I should make my way back to my seat. He seems a little stressed out."

" Yes, you should." Rowan interrupted.

Zach shuffled up the stairs and back to his seat with a flushed, sheepish look on his face. Professor Charles paused his lecture until Zach was seated, making his already roseate face a few shades brighter.

"That guy is the definition of a dork. And really, was that all you had? Comparing yourself to an old lady?" asked Rowan.

"Can you go one day without being president of the peanut gallery?" Halyn asked as she rolled her eyes. Frustrated, she knew that Rowan was right and that she had been too polite to him, but still, she could stick up for herself. She glanced in Zach's direction. He was looking at her and mouthed the words "SORRY". Halyn turned around and started writing without looking back again for the next three hours.

When the bell rang, Halyn waited a few more minutes before leaving the classroom. She didn't want to run into Zach again. She couldn't handle another empty sorry and just wanted to move on with her day. Her plan finally worked after the student who was bribing Professor Charles for a higher quiz grade left (without the extra grade). Even Rowan had escaped before her since her next class was at the other end of campus and she had to rush to get there on time.

Later that afternoon, when Halyn had finished her classes for the day, she thought she should highlight her notes, to make studying for exams easier. She headed to the library and parked herself in her new preferred padded booth overlooking the floor to ceiling fireplace where she relinquished the day's events. She studied for an hour and when her eyes began to cross, she looked up and glanced outside the wall of pane glass windows to her left. The sky was breathtaking. It was a pinkish red and the clouds were spaced perfectly apart to allow the sunset to peek through them. Halyn removed herself from her books to enjoy the horizon when she noticed the poster for the First Year Fling, posted at eye level on the board adjacent to the windows. She debated skipping out on the event, but couldn't disappoint her sister and she really did need a night out. It was college after all. She hated that she had to repetitively convince herself to do anything involving large social gatherings.

She then realized that the date was quickly approaching and she had nothing to wear. Normally, she would just raid her sister's closet because Rowan shopped like it was a sport. Sometimes Halyn would shop with her purely for entertainment. Halyn also realized that the day of the "Fling" was Rowan and her ex's anniversary. She immediately thought of a plan that would be perfect for a distraction from the painful breakup memories, but it was also a plan that would help her own wardrobe dilemma. She decided to plan a day of shopping and pampering earlier in the day before the ball. There were no classes that day and Halyn had originally planned to study, but she knew her brain would be on overload. She couldn't wait to get to Rowan to tell her the plan.

CHAPTER 3

"Do you think this colour would look good on me?" Halyn asked as she pulled a coral low cut blouse from the sale rack.

"You would look good in anything, but that shirt is so last year. It's boring. Everyone has one like that."

"What about this dress for the fling? Halyn pulled out a plain black dress with short sleeves."

"No! You need something sexy, something that screams...I'm here!" she shouted in the quiet store.

Halyn skimmed the room to see if other shoppers were staring. "No Rowan, that's what you need. I like to exude a quiet confidence and you just need to be quiet, in general, especially in a small store like this."

"Come on Halyn! Don't be boring for once and no one cares but you."

" I guess I could use a little sexy in my life. Where else should we look? Have you been to this mall yet?"

"Follow me." Rowan led Halyn through the flood of people along the most modern, clean-cut corridor of stores she had ever seen. They soon walked into a store that was playing classical music and had its own security guards who flanked alongside the golden pillars at the entrance. Halyn couldn't help but comment on the pretentious vibe she was getting. "The slogan for this store should be; Prepare To Feel Really Poor." She commented as they rounded the first pillar towards the dresses.

"And just what are you ladies doing here?" A voice that sounded like nails on a chalkboard echoed from the back corner of the store. " I never thought I would see you two in this store. The perilous sound was moving towards them. "Halyn and Rowan Curtis, fancy meeting you here in this upscale boutique." Halyn rolled her eyes at the sound of Marissa's voice. The shopping trip was now ruined.

" We are shopping. That is what people do in malls, isn't it?" Rowan snapped back.

" Don't waste your energy, Rowan. Let's just go. I wouldn't buy anything here anyway," Halyn whispered.

Rowan and Halyn turned around and headed back out of the entranceway as Marissa chased after them. " Sorry I wasn't at home when you came to pick me up for class."

" That's alright, I forgot anyway. I didn't remember I was supposed to pick you up until I didn't see you in class." Halyn felt guilty for lying, but at the same time, wanted to knock Marissa's ego down a few pegs.

" Really? Oh, I see." Marissa said with a concerned expression. She was processing Halyn's response as embarrassment radiated from her and she looked around to see if anyone had heard the conversation, but luckily for her, no one was around.

" Well, I could use a ride to the Fling tonight. My Benz is still on backorder."

" We are getting a ride with someone else. Sorry"

" I'm sure they wouldn't mind picking me up too."

"Actually, I'm sure they would." Rowan retorted. At that moment, the girls had enough of Marissa Jacobs for one day and they walked out of the store.

Halyn and Rowan made their way back home after they had both successfully found outfits that were perfect for the big night. Halyn went for a strapless, little black dress that was sexy, but not provocative. It was comfortable, which was a welcomed bonus. She chose to accessorize with large chandelier earrings that were certainly out of her comfort zone, a gift from her twin of course, but she revelled in how they reflected the light surrounding her. She planned to borrow a pair of red stilettos from Rowan, which perfectly matched the earrings and her only purse.

The girls started to get ready for the ball while listening to 80's dance music on repeat. Moments later, there was a loud, rapid knock coming from the entrance to Halyn's room. Rowan answered the door, with her hair half up and half curled. A tall, friendly girl was leaning on their door frame. Rowan was taken in by her bubbly personality.

" Hi! My roommate and I were wondering if you are all coming to the Fling tonight?"

" We sure are. Well, my sister and I are anyway. Are you?"

" Yes. My roommates and I are getting ready to head out now. Would you like to come to our dorm and go together? I know we just met, but what better time to make new friends right?

" Right." Rowan looked over her shoulder at her sister who was peeking around the corner of the bathroom. Halyn took a few seconds to assess the new girl and met her contagious smile. "Why not ?" she replied hesitantly. The tall, enthusiastic girl at the door seemed eager for the girls to join them, with a level of excitement like it was Christmas morning. How could she say no? Rowan pulled Halyn down the hall and they walked into a room that smelled of hairspray and last night's pizza. This was a typical college dorm room atmosphere, but Halyn was yet to become accustomed to it.

" Hey, your name is Halyn right?" Said the perky girl.

" Yes, it is," Halyn replied quietly, continuing to assess the new friends they had just made.

"Your name is so unique and beautiful. I'm Lucy and this is Becca." We sit behind you in both Anatomy and Biology. Have you met any new friends here yet? Are you from around here?"

"No, we are not from here. We don't really know anyone either, except our roommates."

" Neither do we. And why aren't you two roommates?" asked Lucy,

" We've lived together our entire lives. We are twins, so that means home life and school life together, all the time. We needed a change." Halyn digressed.

"Well, we are hoping to make some lifelong friends here at Dryden. They say your college friends are the ones you hold on to for life." Becca chimed in.

Rowan rolled her eyes. Bored from all the small talk. "Have you seen any cute guys?" she interjected.

" Is that really the first thing you need to say to someone we first met?" Halyn was not surprised by her sister's vast change in the topic.

"They look like they would know a cute guy if they saw one. That's a compliment by the way." Rowan glanced towards Lucy.

" Well, actually, there are a couple of guys in our class that we are hoping will be here tonight."

" Tell me more," Rowan replied as she sat on the couch with Lucy and Becca. Halyn remained on the floor, listening to the girls talk without engaging. Her break up with Chase was still fresh and the last thing she wanted on her mind was the opposite gender.

After several 90's sitcom reruns, lots of makeup, and boy talk, the girls decided to make their way to the ball. Outside, waiting for them was a pristine white stretch limo that Dryden had sent around campus to pick up all the students. The driver of the car stepped out and greeted the girls, opening the back door and escorting them inside the lavish vehicle. For Halyn, it was completely unexpected and a pleasant surprise. " I need to do this more often." she thought to herself. The limousine glistened in the spotlight of the street lamps illuminating the cobblestone paths and laneways of the college grounds. There were aged cherry trees and pristinely manicured gardens strategically scattered along with the buildings that were so historically enchanted that Halyn had a hard time believing they were real. It was immediately calming and she wished that she could stay there in the limo with only the company of her sister and her new friends for the rest of the night.

The limousine pulled up to a large building displaying a picturesque clock tower, lit up by ambient purple lighting and an archway of balloons leading into the Grand Hall. It was incredibly charming and for the first time since starting the year at Dryden, Halyn felt a hint of excitement.

As the four girls walked into the Grand Hall, they immediately noticed the décor. Crystal ropes hung from the ceiling throughout the entire hall, golden archways were dispersed along the floor and tall floral centerpieces adorned each table. Halyn, Rowan, Lucy, and Becca immediately felt like they were at a Hollywood red carpet event. Halyn looked at the 4-foot tall chocolate fountain and the mermaid ice sculpture that was situated on a round table just as they walked into the hall. It was the focal point of the room. There were fruits on skewers shaped into stars and gourmet desserts lined along rows of tables as far as the eye could see. At the end of the table was a punch station. As she quietly tried to make her way towards the buffet of sweets, Halyn noticed a few of her classmates and suddenly felt a pull on her arm. Rowan, Lucy, and Becca raced her over towards them. "There they are!" exclaimed Becca.

A group of five self-assured young men, all with the same trendy spiked hairstyles strolled into the hall. They sported three-piece suits and as a group, were intimidating and commanded the room. One of them was wearing a florescent pink shirt with a Royal blue suit and another had a top hat on that screamed "Mad Hatter." The Mad Hatter was also carrying a cane but didn't appear to have any trouble walking. If attention was what they were going for, it was working. Halyn was perplexed. " Isn't it supposed to be a black and white affair? And why is everyone in the room turning their heads to swoon over this overrated group of testosterone?" She whispered to Rowan.

As Halyn studied the wolf pack slowly, her eyes widened at the sight of her hit and run assailant. He was not wearing a top hat or a shirt that required sunglasses, however, he was stylish, yet carried a quiet confidence. At first glance, Halyn was enraged, so she quickly shifted her focus back to her new friends, turning her back to Zach Payne and his pack. She was happy to have met Lucy and Becca as she felt more confident with them accompanying her, especially now that he had shown up. Not that she should be surprised, it was an event for all first year students after all. She decided to put his presence to the back of her mind.

Halyn was eyeing up the sweets table when Lucy chimed in. " I'm going to get some fruit from the chocolate fountain and some drinks from the punch station. Would you like some?"

"I'll come with you," Halyn exclaimed as she bounded to the chocolate fountain with Lucy, creating another distraction for herself from the wolf pack. She was in awe of the artwork in front of her. The food was assembled into masterpieces, strategically and meticulously placed to entice even those without a sweet tooth. She was picking up a cupcake when she felt a tap on her shoulder. It startled her so much, that she last her grip on the cupcake, and soon, blue icing created a trail along the front of her new black dress. She looked up to see Zach, staring at her soiled chest. She instantly noticed the mortified expression on his face. "I am ....so....sorry." He said, embarrassed yet again.

As Halyn began to clean off the front of her dress, she noticed that Zach was still staring at her. She looked up at him annoyed. At that moment, he must have realized that he wasn't doing anything productive and flagged down a server walking by.

"Please get this beautiful lady a clean cloth". Halyn smiled sheepishly, and reluctantly.

"I'm very sorry. I feel like we have gotten off on the wrong foot yet again. He gathered as much confidence as he could, to further carry on the conversation.

"You think?" Halyn retorted
Zach smiled. "Can we start again?"

"I didn't know we had started in the first place, " said Halyn, her eyes reduced to half their size as she stared him down.

" You're a sarcastic one aren't you?"

" At your service."

The server returned momentarily, handing her a warm, wet cloth. Halyn gratefully accepted the towel from the server wiped most of the blue icing off her dress and sharply grabbed her purse. She looked up at Zach and for a moment, she felt his angst. " Thanks for getting me a towel." She said nervously. "I'm going to bring what's left of my desserts back to my sister and friends. It was nice to see you again." Halyn walked confidently back towards Lucy, Becca, and Rowan, hoping that no one would notice the wet, faint blue stain along the midline of her dress.

"What happened to you?" Asked Rowan.

"You don't want to know," Halyn replied bitterly.

Finally, the music picked up and the girls needed to work off some of the unnecessary sugar they had just consumed. They danced without a care for most of the night, enjoyed the photo booth and the limbo contest, which Rowan won. She wasn't afraid to show off her flexibility or her undergarments for that matter. Halyn was happy that she had met some new friends. They were genuinely hitting it off and she started to feel that the school year ahead might be better than she had anticipated.

As the night was coming to an end, Halyn noticed that Lucy was waiting in the hall with her jacket on, in some sort of serious conversation with Zach, who also appeared to be ready to leave. Lucy had mentioned that she would wait for her and Rowan at the end of the night. It was nice to see that she was loyal to her word even after the few drinks she snuck into the hall. But why was Zach there? She walked with Rowan to get her jacket when Lucy approached her. " Zach is going to hitch a ride with us. Is that ok?"

"I guess so but doesn't he just live a couple of blocks away?"

Lucy appeared to be trying to find her words. "Um yes, but it's cold out and he doesn't have anyone to walk with."

"Hi, Halyn." Zach appeared from behind Becca, waving nervously.

The five of them walked over to the limo and squeezed in with Zach sitting in the middle of the five girls.

"Where did your wolf pack go?" asked Halyn?

"Wolf pack?" Zach laughed. "You ARE a sarcastic one. I like that. They left early because they wanted to go to some club downtown."

"Even the guy in the top hat? Why didn't you go?"

Zach smirked. "That's Josh....and the club isn't my scene."

And just like that, it was the first time Halyn was semi-charmed by Zach Payne. She was also not enamoured by smoke infested clubs where everyone felt like they were in a can of sardines. They drove down a long driveway to a large stone building. They passed a sign that read Eagan Residence.

"You live here?" Rowan asked in her inebriated astonishment. Halyn soon learned that Rowan had clearly found some spiked punch at some point near the end of the night.

"Yes, it's one of the male only residences. The building next door is the really nice one though. It's called Guildwood. Thanks for keeping me company on the ride. You saved me from being eaten by a coyote." Zach proceeded to laugh at his own joke. Halyn found it endearing and dorky at the same time.

" Well, have a good night." Halyn abruptly escorted Zach out of the car as the limo came to a stop in front of Eagan. All she could think about was getting into her bed and sleeping until noon the next day.

As Zach walked towards the illuminated front entrance of the residence, Rowan mumbled under her breath. " He so likes you Halyn."

"No, he doesn't. I don't even know the guy and he almost hit me with his car remember? Not to mention, he's the cause of a trip to the dry cleaners tomorrow.

" He certainly does," Lucy exclaimed in agreement with Rowan. Lucy had been into the same punch as Rowan." He told me himself. Although he was trying to keep it cool. That's what we were talking about at the end of the night. That's why he wanted a ride and he feels embarrassed by his clumsiness, but he also didn't fail to mention something intriguing."

" Oh yeah, and what's that?

" That he thinks it all happened for a reason."

CHAPTER 4

Halyn lay in her bed for over an hour, replaying the conversation she had in the car with Lucy and Rowan, trying to understand how Zach could possibly think that some kind of relationship could potentially develop between them. All she knew of Zach was that he was clumsy, didn't like clubs, and couldn't drive. But as she thought more about his demeanour and stopped ruminating about the latter, she saw something different. He did compliment her and say she was beautiful. He had been nothing but polite, gracious, and humble, careful not to embarrass her or make her feel uncomfortable. She hadn't noticed how attractive he was until now. The image she had in her mind of a tall, gentle, dark-haired, blue-eyed man was starting to make her internal wall crumble ever so slowly. " Should I be less critical of him? Should I give him the chance to redeem himself?" She thought out loud, as she slowly reopened her eyes for the day. She was still wearing her purple flannel pyjamas and didn't plan to take them off for the rest of the day. As she logged onto the computer to work on one of her assignments, she noticed that she had two friend requests and a message from Rowan. She checked the message first.

"HEY! Wake up! Are you seriously still sleeping? You didn't even have a cocktail last night. By the way, Lucy and Becca are going to add you."

Halyn then proceeded to check her add friend requests. The first was from Lucy, which was not surprising and the second was from Becca. She added them to her list of contacts and Lucy was online.

"Hey" last night was fun right? I'm already counting down the days until we can do it again. I'm so happy to have made new friends already!"

"Yes, I had a good time. It was great to meet you and Becca."

" Same. Do you want to study this afternoon at the library?"

" I could go for some company while I study. I like the floor with the fireplace."

" Me too. So I added Zach, he's wondering if he can add you too."

Halyn felt a bit annoyed but then thought about the conversation she had with herself just a few minutes earlier. Would this open a can of worms she didn't want to get into? She was single and happy to be and certainly didn't want to lead anyone on. She abruptly stopped her thoughts, shaking her head, and decided it was best to not over-analyze the situation. All Lucy had said was that he liked her. For all she knew, he could be in a relationship, or could simply be trying to beg for further forgiveness.

The friend request screen then popped up. She felt butterflies in the pit of her stomach. "Don't over-think Halyn." She said to herself as she quickly pressed the "accept" key. Zach's name popped up, followed by a message. With a trembling grip, she clicked and opened the message.

"Hi Halyn, did you get a good sleep?"

"She hesitated before replying."

"Yes, thank you. I managed to settle quickly and slept in a little this morning."

"Great. What are your plans for this afternoon? I guess it is almost noon."

"Why is he asking? Does he want to make plans?" She asked herself remembering that luckily, she already had plans to study later at the library.

"I'm heading to the library to study with Rowan and Lucy. Midterms are in a week and I've barely studied."

"I'm planning to study tonight as well. Don't think I can get around to it this afternoon though. I need to fix my car door. I realized that my brakes are shot. That's

why I almost hit you a few weeks ago. I'm sorry about that, and I'm sorry about last night's mishap too."

Halyn's hands trembled again. Every time she remembered the incident with the car, it made her nauseous and she just wished she could remove it from her memory. Maybe this conversation would put the issue to rest. She could just accept his apology, and they could all move on. So reluctantly, she did just that.

"It's in the past. I'm happy to hear you figured out the problem with your car though. I'm going to get ready to head to the library now. I hope you have a good day."

"I'll see you in class tomorrow?"

"Bright and early."

After a long pause, he sent her a smiley face emoji. Halyn jumped in the shower and put on the most comfortable outfit she could find. "So much for a pyjama day." She thought as she pictured herself nestled by the fireplace in the library with a comfy sweater dress, a coffee, and sneakers. It would have to do. If slippers were allowed, she would wear them too. She threw her hair in a messy bun, grabbed her over-sized bag, and sauntered out the door. She was going to have to pick up lunch at the café because she was running late.

She met the girls outside the library. Even from a distance, both Lucy and Rowan looked as though they were going to fall on the floor. They were clutching giant bottles of water with no coffee in sight.

"Rough morning ladies?" Halyn asked as she approached them, their faces, pale and gaunt. Rowan gave her a sarcastic, unimpressed glare. "Sorry. It was just a question."

"Do we have to study?" Rowan whined with a raspy voice.

"Well you don't have to, but I am" replied Halyn.

"I have to," Lucy responded with a strained voice. "I'm one step away from flunking this class, so I need some tutoring and someone to crack the whip on me." Rowan and Halyn giggled.

"Oh, you know what I mean." Lucy flushed

The girls stumbled up the library stairs and took their places in Halyn's usual booth. Halyn got right into studying, with her highlighter almost burning holes in the pages of her anatomy textbook. After they had finished reviewing their notes, Halyn looked up to see Marissa in the distance, soaking in the praise she was receiving from a group of desperate young men practically drooling on her notes, each of them trying to outwit one another for her attention. Halyn rolled her eyes.

"Do you know her?" Asked Lucy. "She's so pretty."

"No she isn't." snapped Rowan.

Lucy's eyes grew four sizes and she became beet red in the face. Halyn rolled her eyes again. "

Sorry, Lucy. What Rowan meant to say is that yes we know her. We knew her growing up and trust us, the beauty is all on the outside. We used to be friends, but that was a long time ago and we are very different people now. Marissa met Lucy's glance, smiled playfully at the boys, and fanned them away. They reluctantly obeyed and one of them almost walked into a bookshelf with his eyes still fixated on her. She walked over to the girls who were desperately attempting to avoid her as she approached. She slammed her textbook on the table and took a seat beside Lucy.

" I couldn't help but notice your new friend staring at me. I'm Marissa." She reached her hand out to shake Lucy's. Lucy shook her hand and then quickly glanced at Rowan who could cut a hole in someone's heart with her fierce glare. Lucy could smell the tension and she quickly wanted to break the ice.

" I'm Lucy. I believe we are in some of the same classes."

" Hmm, I never noticed you," Marissa replied pretentiously, as she applied her rosy pink lip gloss.

Rowan was desperately holding back contempt and trying to keep herself quiet. Marissa had only been sitting with them for a mere matter of minutes and Rowan was bursting at the seams.

"Well, I came over to let you ladies know that I am having a house party the Friday night after midterms and you all made the list."

"We feel so honoured," replied Rowan sarcastically.

" Sounds great!" Lucy was smiling from ear to ear. "Can I bring anything?"

" Bring anything? Honey, I'm having it catered." Marissa picked up her tan coloured designer bag and strutted away in her four-inch leather heels, her long red hair bouncing effortlessly along her slender torso.

" She seems nice," Lucy said sheepishly. Halyn and Rowan stared at her, before looking down at their notes for the next three hours.

Midterms seemed to go fairly well for Halyn. She was sure she aced a couple of them and felt a huge wave of relief as she left her last exam until she thought about Marissa's party that was to take place in a few hours. She was happy that she would have friends there with her to ease off some of the awkward tension. Rowan, Lucy, and Becca were all going to be joining her and they had decided that they would all get ready together and go out for dinner before the party. That was always Halyn's favourite part of a night out. She could often do without the late nights and sweaty crowds. Rowan had agreed to go to Marissa's party when she heard that many of the first and second-year guys would be there. Halyn had agreed to go only if the other girls could come along with them. And with this, they compromised. Still, Halyn would rather just go for a nice dinner and then curl up in her comfy pyjamas while watching a movie with the girls.

As Halyn was leaving the hall where the exams took place, she heard Zach's voice and promptly started walking faster towards the door. " Halyn!". She couldn't escape now. She stopped, took a deep breath, and turned to face Zach and Eric who were coming towards her.

" How did it go? The exam I mean."

" I think it went well thank you. I was stumped on the last question, but I think I managed to answer all the others with some confidence. How about you?"

Zach smiled adoringly at Halyn while he answered in a raspy, exhausted voice. "For the most part well, at least I think I did well. You never can tell sometimes. I'm just happy it is over."

"Me too." Halyn met Zach's infectious smile.

" Are you going to Marissa's party tonight." He asked, his voice more upbeat this time.

Halyn wanted to say no, that she would rather climb in a dumpster, but alas he would inevitably see her there tonight. " Yes. I'm going with some of the girls from class."

" Rowan and Lucy?"

" Yes, and Becca. We are getting together really soon, so I should probably get home and get my place ready. I'll see you later." She started to walk away and immediately loathed how awkward she felt when she talked to Zach and to make matters worse, she heard him following her out of the building.

"I'm looking forward to seeing you tonight. And the answer was potassium chloride." Zach gave her a nervous glance, his teeth clenched.

"I'm sorry?"

"The answer to the last question on the exam. Potassium chloride."

Reading the apprehensive expression on his face, Halyn smiled back at him and walked out the door. Relieved, he winked at her and started walking in the opposite direction.

"Huh" Halyn expressed to herself.

On the walk home, Halyn was trying to figure out why Zach continued to make her feel both uncomfortable yet empathetic. She had forgiven him for both the car and cupcake incidents, and really at the end of the day, they weren't a big deal. Maybe it was because he was always so persistent to talk to her. But this didn't make any sense either. He was always kind to her and now she honestly had no reason to dislike him.

When she arrived at her dorm, Ellie was nowhere to be found which made Halyn pleasantly surprised. She had the room to herself and proceeded to put on her music and try on a few outfits for the evening ahead. She put on her boy band playlist and began tidying up. An hour went by quickly, and soon there was a knock on the door. Rowan came in with both Becca and Lucy and the girls immediately began plugging in curling irons and putting on makeup.

"I brought a bunch of clothes," Lucy said. "Feel free to borrow them, ladies. Halyn, I have something special for you though." Lucy pulled out a beautiful V-neck, skin-tight red dress and held it up towards Halyn. Her jaw dropped. "That's for me?"

"Yes! It will look amazing on you. You have the perfect figure for it."

"Oh wow, Halyn! You would look amazing in that. You have to wear it with your sparkly shoes that I bought you on our birthday. You've never worn them. I've been keeping tabs."

When it came to fashion, Rowan's approval meant a lot to Halyn, so she knew the red dress was a winner. Halyn loved the dress but had never worn anything so bright, so bold or tight for that matter. She enjoyed the idea of getting pampered but also thought that this was a classic example of a passive-aggressive intervention.

"What is this all about?" she asked.

" We just want you to look beautiful" replied Lucy, slyly.

Halyn didn't want to ask any more questions. She reluctantly agreed to let the girls play stylist on her. In the end, they were having fun and it was making them all feel like gracious humanitarians. They curled her naturally wavy brown hair in long loose curls and even gave her fake eyelashes, which were incredibly uncomfortable. But when she looked in the mirror, she felt beautiful and pleasantly surprised with how comfortable her dress and shoes were.

Pulling up into the driveway of Marissa's lake house was like making a grand entrance onto sacred grounds. Halyn was mesmerized by the ambient lighting along the driveway. Marissa had outdone herself with decorations too. Flower balls and lanterns hung from the trees and there were dapper valet parking attendants. If Halyn didn't know any better, she would have thought she was going to a royal wedding instead of a house party. The girls felt like celebrities as they walked out of the taxi. Men in black bow ties and white gloves handed out champagne in diamond-encrusted flutes. The doorman took their jackets and placed them delicately on a coat hanger that stood under an enormous crystal chandelier. Inside, the music was loud and the food looked like it had come straight off a five- star cruise ship. Halyn couldn't wait to get to the sweets table again.

Marissa came prancing to the door, champagne in hand, attitude in check. As always, she looked stunning and exuded arrogance. She wore a long fuchsia maxi dress with a turquoise statement necklace. Her hair and makeup appeared to be done professionally. Halyn was certain it was done by a celebrity stylist. She smiled and led the girls inside to the large chef's kitchen. From the kitchen, there was a spacious, and tranquil deck with chaise lounge chairs that looked onto a pristine, calm lake.

The girls quickly separated, exploring the home and the grounds. Halyn was interested in the picturesque scenery outside. Lucy was entertaining another group of girls and Rowan was hunting for the wolf pack. Halyn sat in one of the lounge chairs underneath a state of the art heat lamp and couldn't help but feel slightly jealous that Marissa had this stellar home and view. Halyn always saw herself living on the ocean or somewhere warm and tropical. This is what she hoped for once her career took off. She would have a family and they would live just like this, with water out the windows and trees flowing in the wind, minus the men in black ties and servants.

Halyn was sipping a lemonade peacefully when she caught a glance of Lucy and Zach from the corner of her eye. She was starting to think that Lucy had a thing for him since they were always chatting, and engaged in profound conversation. Halyn noticed that even though Zach was smiling, he also looked a little nervous. She first noticed him remove his sunglasses as they revealed his blue eyes. He had his light brown hair spiked up perfectly and his outfit was impressively color co-ordinated. Halyn shook her head and looked out onto the water, having the urge to make her way closer to the shoreline. She made her way down the rocky bank, towards the shore. When she reached the water, she began running her feet through the miniature waves along the private beach. "Marissa has her own beach." Halyn's thoughts became childishly envious. While sauntering along the sand, she stumbled into Lucy who had made her way onto the shore as well, somehow still wearing three-inch heels. They both eyed up the paddleboat beside them.

"Hey, Lucy. Want to go for a paddleboat ride?"

Lucy looked up towards the house at Zach and then back towards the paddle boat. "Yes, I do in fact," she replied as if she had just come up with the brilliant idea herself.

"Do you have a thing for Zach?" Halyn asked nervously as she pulled the paddleboat along the sand and into the shallow water.

" No. We are just friends." Lucy removed her heels and tugged on the other side of the boat until it was completely in the water.

" You two always seem to be having such important conversations," Halyn said as they climbed in, Lucy taking charge of the steering handle.

Lucy looked at Halyn and smiled. "We do have important conversations....and they are about you. Let's get this boat going and we can chat. It will be nice!"

The girls put their life jackets on and Halyn started to feel a pit in her stomach. Was she really being that standoffish towards Zach? She started to feel moderately guilty and thought it may be a good idea to apologize to him when she got back to the house. As the boat began to glide along the water, Halyn felt relaxed and took a moment to gaze at the calm lake, thinking that maybe it wasn't such a bad idea that she came to Marissa's party. The breeze was refreshing and crisp while the sun was just starting to set, leaving a graceful pink hue in the sky. The girls closed their eyes and took time to enjoy the moment. The silence was soon broken by Lucy's voice. " He adores you, you know."

"Who does?" Halyn asked, although she already knew the answer.

"Don't play dumb" Lucy retorted. "Zach does. That's what we are always talking about. He always asking questions about you and trying to find ways to get your attention. It's like his mission right now." Halyn took a moment to process this information again. She didn't know how to respond.

" He thinks you're beautiful, and smart, and would make a great mom someday." Lucy laughed

" Whoa slow down! Children are nowhere in my near future."

" Well, I don't think he means like next week. I think it's just in your character and I agree with him. You have some nurturing qualities. I wouldn't want to be your friend if you didn't have those kind and genuine qualities." Lucy said blushing.

" Thanks. That's nice of you to say. It's just that I recently ended a serious relationship and I think that I need some time to myself for a while."

" Understandable. You're a heart breaker. In any event, he wants to ask you out, but is afraid you will chew his face off."

" Smart man," Halyn replied sarcastically. Lucy focused in on Halyn's eyes as if trying to figure out if she was serious or not.

" I'm kidding. I think he's ok, I just don't want to be in a relationship right now."

" Well, I sort of, kind of told him that I would bring you back to the house to hang out together. He's probably wondering where we are right now since I was heading to the beach to come and bring you to him."

"I'm glad you warned me first, but I don't know what to say to him."

" Just come with me and I will keep the conversation rolling," Lucy replied confidently.

The girls headed back towards the party as the sun was almost completely set. Lucy placed the life jackets on the boat and led Halyn up the long flight of stairs to the back deck of the house. There was a large crowd now and the girls quickly realized it was going to be a challenge for them to find everyone. They spotted Rowan first, with her arm around a brute football player. Halyn only knew he played football because he was wearing the school's leather team jacket. Halyn and Lucy studied their body language for a moment. Rowan was the ultimate hair twister. When she was nervous or flirting, she would twist her hair around her finger until it turned blue. Football player was pretending to pay attention to Rowan but was easily distracted by almost every other female that walked by, eyeing each of them down and even winking at some. Rowan appeared to be oblivious to this. Halyn recognized that she had to intervene. She walked over to them and politely grabbed Rowan's hand. "Excuse me. I just have to talk to my sister." She pulled Rowan around the kitchen and into the marble flanked hallway. Rowan became infuriated. " What are you doing?"

" I'm saving you. That guy has player written all over him and not just football player."

"I didn't need to be saved Halyn. Worry about yourself. I don't need to be chaperoned. "

" He was staring at every other girl that walked by you. He was all but drooling all over them."

" Well, that's for me to figure out. Not you. You have to stop being such a prude. And honestly, it isn't like you're a relationship expert."

Halyn felt insulted and mortified. Anyone and everyone standing in the hallway heard their conversation. Halyn removed herself from her sister's harsh words and found Lucy, who was still frantically trying to hunt down Zach. With Zach nowhere to be found, Lucy and Halyn went outside onto the deck to sit and watch the last moments of the sunset. Halyn reflected on her conversation, or better yet argument with Rowan.

"Was I acting like a chaperone? Is Rowan now able to make her own mistakes and learn from them?" She asked Lucy, holding back tears.

"She's her own person, and a feisty one at that. I would leave it to her to figure it out. If she's in any kind of immediate danger, that's when we step in." replied Lucy honestly.

As much as Halyn didn't want to admit it, she knew she had to let her sister learn the hard way. She sat in a lounge chair on the deck for a while, deep in thought when she heard Marissa's shrieking laugh. Halyn caught Marissa with her arm around Zach out of the corner of her eye. She was emphatically bragging about her family inheritance and all the luxury homes and theatres they owned all over the globe.

Halyn couldn't stand it anymore and was about to go in to find Becca with Lucy when she took another glance at Zach, unable to take her eyes off of him. At that very moment, it hit her. It hit her like a tonne of bricks. She loved the way the corner of his mouth lifted and revealed a small dimple when he smiled, and how his eyes were so incredibly crystal clear. She melted as she admired the way he leaned against the wall, placing the palm of his hand behind his neck. Unexpectedly, she became jealous of Marissa's boisterous flirting. Both she and Lucy could tell by his body language that he was just as annoyed by Marissa as they were. It also suddenly occurred to Halyn that he appeared humble and kind, even though Marissa wasn't deserving of such a modest response.

Panic filled Halyn's chest and she leaned into the wall, her heart pounding at the overwhelming realization that it was these emotions she had been fighting off all along. Now that she allowed herself to let her guard down, she was able to identify the source of her awkwardness around him. All she had to do was admit to herself that she was attracted to Zach. He was beautiful and captivating, a catch for any girl at the party. And with that, he needed to be saved from Marissa. Halyn stood up straight and smoothed her red dress. She shook out her hair and reached into her jewelled clutch for her lip gloss. Never in a million years did she think she would reapply lip gloss for a guy, but here she was, sweaty palms and all. Confidently, she walked over towards Zach. With each step, she was getting more and more nervous. When she was within earshot of him and was about to call his name, Marissa suddenly leaned in and kissed him. Halyn's heart sank and the expression on her face mirrored it, because, at that moment, Zach turned and saw Halyn standing behind Marissa, his heart sinking when he realized she had witnessed the unwanted exchange. Halyn turned around briskly and walked towards the washroom when Zach grabbed her arm gently.

" Hey." He said gently, his voice angelic and patient.

"Hi." She replied, her voice quivering. It was the second time she was mortified that night.

"Were you coming to talk to me?" he asked.

"I was, but you were a little busy."

"I'm never too busy for you."

Halyn smiled at him and looked into his eyes. They were as blue as any eyes could be and she felt like they were piercing through her heart. She caved and gave into his smile. "I'm sorry, it's just that you were talking to Marissa and she kissed you and I didn't want to interrupt. I didn't know you even knew each other, let alone interested in each other."

"I'm not interested in her Halyn. She is certainly looking for some fun tonight. I can tell she likes the attention and she doesn't do it for me." Halyn felt relieved and nervous again all at the same time. She didn't want to get ahead of herself and tried to collect her thoughts.

"Do you want to go outside by the fire?" Zach asked

"Which one?" Halyn joked

Zach smiled at Halyn and was attracted to her sense of humour. "Whichever you like best."

They walked down towards the beach. There were many people crowded around the fires and neither Halyn nor Zach were looking for a crowd at the moment. "I have an idea." She said to him. Halyn gathered some wood, a lighter from a lonely smoker on the beach, a blanket, and some paper from her purse. She grabbed Zach's hand and started to run. They ran into the thick flock of trees that lined the property onto a large flat rock that overlooked the lake. It was calm and quiet, and it was just what they were both looking for. Halyn began to make a fire and when the flames started to successfully crackle, Zach couldn't help but comment on how impressed he was.

"You have some experience with campfires I see. Girl Scouts?"

"Maybe." She smirked timidly
"It's ok, I'll only tell a hundred people."

Halyn found herself easily falling for Zach's quirky sense of humour. Everything about him was becoming more captivating by the second. They spread out the plush blanket and sat on the grass surrounding the fire. It was a warm evening with the humidity lingering in the air. They sat with an arm length distance between their shoulders, listening to the calm waves hitting the rocks below their feet, not saying a word. Zach gazed at Halyn while she stared at the fire with a confident yet genial smile on his face. He decided to break the ice.

"Why the sudden change of heart?" He asked honestly.

Halyn kept her eyes on the waves. She didn't know how to answer his question because she wasn't able to answer it herself. She realized that it was likely not a change of heart, instead it was a realization that she had been in denial all this time. From the first time she saw Zach, she ignored the butterflies, the loss of words, and couldn't get him off her mind. " I don't know. I just thought maybe we could have the chance to get to know each other."

Zach looked at her, smiling from ear to ear. "I'd like that. You are mysterious to me. I find you hard to read."

"Most people do." She replied with a snicker under her breath. "I'm pretty guarded."

" I want to know who Halyn Curtis is. What can you tell me?"

Halyn sighed heavily. " Well, I was born 8 minutes after my sister and grew up in a small city approximately three hours north of here. I was a dancer and a swimmer and I have always loved school, and I love being here, introverted in the outdoors, close to water. I'm quiet, a bookworm and loyal.

" From that description, I take it you aren't one for late nights and parties?"

" Well, it depends on your description of a party. I like to entertain and be with friends and socialize, but I'm not a fan of the clubs or house parties all that much. Hence why I am out here with you."

" Neither am I really, I much prefer this scenery any day. I'll never turn down a concert or traveling to somewhere exotic though. Those are opportunities you may never have a chance to experience again."

Halyn looked over at Zach who was still fiercely staring into her eyes. She could feel the warmth and desire in his and quickly looked back at the fire.

" What about you. What was Zach's life like?' she asked him.

" I grew up just outside of New York City. It's a little place called Irvington. It's beautiful and relaxing, but also just a hop, skip, and a jump away from Manhattan. You never feel like you're in the city when you are there, but I do have to say, I love New York and the hustle and bustle of it all. I plan to work there someday and take over my dad's business. I have an older brother and my parents split up last year."

"I'm sorry." Halyn felt a pang of guilt.

" It's OK, it was for the best. My dad was never home and my mom just fell out of love with him. It was a toxic environment in some ways." Halyn felt herself wanting to quickly change the subject. " What are your interests?" she asked him.

"My interests?" He paused with a sly grin teetering from the corner of his mouth, exposing the dimple that Halyn found irresistible. "Real estate, music, and you."

She couldn't help but smile back. She could feel her face flush and tried to make it discreet. " Those are all very different things" she replied inching closer to him.

" My dad owns a real estate company, I've played the guitar since childhood, and you are the most beautiful girl I have ever laid eyes on."

Zach's charm and wit won her over and Halyn could no longer resist the temptation and tension that was so heavy between them. She leaned in and kissed him, surprised at her impulsivity. In the moment, the connection was undeniable. It was more authentic than any moment Halyn ever had with anyone else. Zach opened his eyes, smiled, and let out a sigh of relief. He was happy that she initiated their first kiss. He also felt like he could let his guard down. He now knew that she was feeling the same way he had been feeling for weeks. Since meeting Halyn, he couldn't take his eyes off of her. He was irrefutably drawn to her natural beauty and humble demeanour. She was mystifying and adorable at the same time. And although precarious, he thought that the car incident was a test of fate. He took off his coat and put it around Halyn's shoulders. He pulled her in close, and they sat on their blanket by the lake for hours talking about nothing and everything, and soon they fell asleep in each other's arms.

The next morning, Zach dropped Halyn off at her dorm. She felt slightly ashamed wearing her clothes from the night before. She stepped out of the car that almost hit her a few weeks prior, but this time, she had a very different feeling about being in its presence. It belonged to Zach and he had built it with his own hands, a true sign of his amazing work ethic and talent. She was infatuated, and couldn't wait to see him again.

" I will call you tomorrow", he said as he kissed her on the forehead.

" I'd love that." He closed the door behind her. "Chivalry isn't dead after all," she whispered as she motioned up the stairs to her dorm.

CHAPTER 5

Halyn looked at her phone and smiled as a message from Zach appeared on the bright screen. Her eyes still had not adjusted to waking up. She and Zach had been dating for several weeks and she was perfectly smitten. Waking up every morning, knowing she would get to spend the day with Zach at school was making her happier than she had ever been. Waking up early every Monday morning, was no longer a dreaded chore. He showered her with compliments and frequently went out of his way, impressing her with small gestures. He left notes on her desk at school, while she left notes on his car. He made her lunches for school and frequently stopped off at the library with a latte for her while she studied. He held her hand when she was nervous before a test and let her choose the movies they would watch since she liked romantic comedies and he liked horror flicks.

"I miss you already. Can you come to my place tonight? I can't wait until Monday."

He had just dropped her off the day prior,

after a full day of hiking and dinner. Her mind was racing at the thought of seeing him again and she hadn't been to his home yet, so in anticipation, she didn't hesitate to respond.

"Yes, I can't wait either."

"See you in an hour?"

" I'm going to need a bit more time, but I'll see you as soon as I'm ready. How about 8 o'clock?"

"Perfect. I'll see you soon."

    Halyn sent a message to Rowan, Lucy and Becca as quickly as her fingers could type. She needed their help. For the first time in a long time, she wanted to look her best for Zach when she showed up at his place. She also wanted to pick him up a gift. "That's what people do when going to someone's home for the first time right?" She thought to herself. So she needed ample time to get ready and come up with the perfect gift idea. Then she remembered something that would be perfect for him. She reached under her bed and pulled out a long plastic bin. She rummaged through it pushing away a large pile of sentimental items. Inside a small blue velvet box were two green guitar picks. On them was an eye sporting long eyelashes. Her Grand-dad had given them to her a few years back. He had told her that he had the guitar picks designed when she was a toddler. "My granddaughters have the most beautiful eyes with eyelashes for days." He told them.

When Halyn's Grand-dad was too frail to play the guitar anymore, he had requested if she could hold on to them as a family keepsake. Halyn always had a special relationship with her Grand-dad. He was the voice of reason within the family and kept the unit afloat. Despite their differences, he knew how to keep the family connection somehow alive and well. Halyn found a silver ribbon around an old gift bag and tied it in a bow around the velvet box and placing it delicately into her purse along with her favourite lip gloss. She put on her red blouse, borrowed a pair of subtle diamond earrings from Becca, and a pair of skinny jeans that fit perfectly into her knee-high black leather boots. "Thank goodness for friends with fashion sense." She thought

Rowan had curled Halyn's hair and Lucy gave her a glamorous yet non-exaggerated smoky eye before she gathered her belongings and headed out the door. As she moved swiftly through the hall and into the entranceway, she saw a small black car that appeared utterly similar to Zach's. It wasn't long before she realized it was, in fact, his car parked discretely outside her building. She walked faster towards the door and peered down the resplendent staircase leading up to the entrance of the building. At the bottom of the stairs stood Zach, striking as ever, smiling directly at her with a bouquet of her favourite flowers in his outstretched hand. Gerber daisies and lattes were both undeniable ways to her heart. He had figured this out quickly. She was over the moon, gratified to see him at the bottom of the stairs. The light hit his face just enough for him to appear out of the darkness. She immediately had butterflies in the pit of her stomach and ran down the stairs to meet his outstretched arms. He had driven over to campus to pick her up.

"I'm so pleasantly surprised. I thought I was going to meet you at your place." She said as she gazed into his eyes locking her arms around his broad shoulders. He kept one hand around her waist and moved a curly tuft of hair out from in front of her eyes. He wanted to see her entire face.

" I thought I would surprise you and come pick you up. I'm the one with a car, just in case you forgot I had it. " He laughed as if he were proud of his own joke.

"How could I forget?" She looked down at the flowers and giggled. " I'll cancel my taxi then."

"Yes please do. And here you go. I got these for you. Your sister mentioned they were your favourite flowers a few weeks ago in class and I remembered. "

Halyn was surprisingly impressed with his effort and the gesture won Zach some serious brownie points. She leaned in and kissed him briefly. He pulled her back in and kissed her again, except this time slowly and with intention. As they reluctantly let go of each other, Zach led

Halyn to the passenger side door and opened it, holding the flowers for her as she got in the car. As he was about to reach for his door, he looked up to a nearby window to see three heads peering out, taking in the show. Zach smiled and re-assuringly waved to them knowing that they were looking out for their girl.

Halyn walked up to the residence where Zach lived with his three other roommates. She could hear video games and shameless grunting from the second floor. "Definitely a guy's place." she thought to herself. Then from a distance, she heard a gruff voice.

" Hey Zach, is that the girl you almost hit with your car?"

"Shut up Josh!" Zach sighed heavily and led Halyn inside.

T heir apartment was pleasantly tidy and smelled of laundry detergent and aftershave, a stark combination, but still not so bad for a house full of college boys. To the right of the door was a poster of Bob Marley above a leather bench with coats and beer cases on top of it. As she walked down the hall and up the stairs, Halyn knew she was getting closer to the main living area as she could hear the faint sound of a violent video game getting louder. She turned the corner to see Eric and Josh in their jeans, with no shirts, two bags of popcorn, and what appeared to be a pizza that was a few hours old in front of them.

"Guys, this is Halyn." Zach introduced them, embarrassed that they did not look up from the television screen. Eric grabbed a piece of pizza, and then lazily glanced towards Halyn. "Nice to see you again. Mi Casa, Su Casa! Want some pizza?"

"No thank you. I just ate."

Josh finally looked up from his game, when he lost to Eric. He had a stocky build and lifted far too much weight at the gym for his body dimensions. He stood up to shake Halyn's hand and she quickly realized that he was the lone wolf pack member wearing the top hat at the Fling. She giggled in her head and shook his hand.

"Come this way, I'll give you a tour," Zach clasped his fingers through Halyn's feeling her soft palms against his own. He looked down at her chipped nail polish and kissed her hand as they walked through the hall. They finished the tour upstairs where the end of the hall led to the Master bedroom.

"Is this your room?" she asked.

"Indeed it is. It's nothing to brag about, but spacious never the less."

"You say that with so much confidence. And you have your own bathroom and walk-in closet. So not fair for the others".

"Don't feel bad for them. I pay way more, and besides, I also study way more and spend a lot of time at home. The other guys are always out and never come home until the early hours of the morning. It was an easy compromise on their part.

Basically, I guilted them into it."

"Are these your guitars?" Halyn pointed towards the right of his television stand where three guitars lined the wall, strategically placed to be noticed.

" Yes, I've collected them over the years. I prefer this one." Zach picked up a black and silver guitar that had some signatures at the bottom. "It was my Grandfather's. He played with the Beach Boys a couple of times, so they signed it for me.

Halyn appreciated Zach's love for quiet nights, studying, and sentimental memorabilia. She was then reminded of the gift she had put away in her purse. It was the perfect time to give it to him. She rummaged through her purse and then looked up at Zach, staring into his ocean blue eyes. "I have something for you." She said sheepishly.

" For me? Well, come on over here then." Zach led them to a giant gray bean bag chair, large enough to fit an entire family. They both let out a contented sigh when they sat down into the chair, relieved by its comfort. Halyn couldn't help but lean in closely to Zach since the natural contour of the chair made her slide right in next to him.

" This may be a little soon, but I was hoping you would like it. It was my Grand- dad's and I just wanted you to know how much you mean to me. I also know you love music, and so did he. He would appreciate you having it." She pulled the velvet case out of her purse and handed it to Zach. He rotated it in his hands nervously before opening it. "

It's not a ring. You don't need to be nervous. Open it." She was already hesitant that he would think it was too much, too soon. Zach slowly opened the box with a quivering grip.

"He made it for me to keep after he got sick, a family heirloom of sorts." Halyn whispered with what felt like a giant a frog in her throat.

Zach opened the case and smiled with his eyes looking down at the guitar pick. "This is amazing Halyn Its like art. Are you sure I can use it?"

" It is yours. I have another one at home that is exactly the same."

Zach turned towards Halyn, wrapped his palms around her face, and kissed her on the forehead. It was her preferred kind of kiss. There was something beautifully intimate in a forehead kiss. It wasn't the lustful, provocative kind, but rather protective and genuine.

"This is a big step forward," he said, his response surprising her a little.

"Why do you say that?"

"Well, not long ago, you were quite adamant that you were not looking for anything serious. This seems serious to me."

Halyn immediately felt the frog turn into a lump in her throat. She knew it was too soon to gift him with something so sentimental. She became flushed and felt her palms getting clammy. She was unable to find her words to respond to him. Zach noticed she was getting worried. He held her hand and put his other arm around her shoulder. She began to second guess herself, fearing that he simply enjoyed the chase and that now that she had him, he would disappear. Then he leaned in fully and kissed her so passionately that all of Halyn's worries melted away. He was hers and she was his in this moment, and that was all that mattered.

CHAPTER 6

On Monday morning, Zach's desk was empty in anatomy class. Halyn was looking forward to seeing him, and he had never been late before so naturally, she was perplexed by his tardiness. She turned to Rowan who was intricately braiding her hair instead of retrieving her pens and notebook. She whispered anxiously into Rowan's ear. " I don't see Zach. I'm worried something happened."

"Class just started. Who knows, maybe he slept in." Rowan raised a suspicious eyebrow. "You are truly falling for this guy. He can't even be five minutes late without you going all captain obsessive on him. Are you going to give him detention later?" She asked slyly, raising her eyebrows up and down with a witty look on her face.

" Rowan stop patronizing me. I'm honestly worried about him."

"Text him then."

"You know how I feel about texting in class. Besides, if something bad happened, he wouldn't get back to me now anyway. I won't be able to focus if he doesn't show up."

As the lecture went on, Halyn kept glancing towards Zach's empty chair. Eric wasn't in his seat either. She became even more worried and when she couldn't take the unknown any longer, she decided to sneak out of class. Professor Charles caught a glimpse of Halyn leaving. She could see that he was taking note in his mind of her early exit, but she couldn't stand to think that perhaps Zach was in trouble. She texted him twice, but he hadn't replied. Luckily she had taken her bike to school, so she decided to head for his place, anxious about what she may or may not see. She sped into his driveway and came to a sudden halt, parking her bike beside Zach's car. He was home. Just then, her phone vibrated and lit up with Zach's name appearing on the screen.

"I'm sick. I was up all night and just woke up. I'm sorry I didn't message you."

Green face sick emoji*

Relieved, Halyn did not reply and decided to instead surprise him by going in to take care of him. She was already standing at his front door and thought he could probably use a little TLC. She opened the door quietly. "Hello?" she shouted. She heard footsteps descending the stairs at the far end of the hall. As the footsteps slowly made their way closer, Halyn removed her shoes and threw her bag by the door. As she removed her jacket and placed it on the bench full of beer cases, she looked up to see Zach, striking as ever, in only his baggy gray jogging pants. His hair was standing on end and his face pale as a ghost, but still incredibly handsome nonetheless.

"How on earth can you look so good after vomiting and getting no sleep?" She asked genuinely. "It is incredibly unfair. "

"Well, this is a pleasant surprise," Zach said, mustering up as much of a smile as could.

" I was hoping you would think so. How are you feeling?"

"Terrible, but I'm in better spirits now. You look beautiful. I'd come and kiss you, but you don't want whatever I have." He glanced at his watch. "Aren't you supposed to be in anatomy?"

" Yes, but I was worried about you. I couldn't concentrate and Professor Charles was reviewing everything we learned last week. I'm not missing much. I've looked over those notes twice already."

" Of course you have." Zach let out a devious chuckle. He looked over at Halyn shyly while he wiped sweat beads off his forehead. "I'm burning up, but strangely enough, I also have the chills. Are you staying for a bit? I won't get too close, and maybe it would be a good idea to stay out of my bedroom." He was embarrassed, but happy Halyn had come by to keep him company.

Halyn moved in closer towards Zach without touching him. As much as she wanted to jump into his arms, she knew it would be better in the long run to keep a healthy distance. " I'm going to take care of you today. What's first? Soup or a sports drink? You need to replenish those electrolytes."

" You're such a nerd," he said. "But I love you, I mean, I love it…..yes… it." Zach choked on his words, and an awkward silence settled between them.

Halyn felt his hesitation and she led Zach to the lazy boy in the TV room. She plugged in a heated blanket and placed a box of soda crackers on a TV tray beside him. On it, she also placed a glass of water, the remote control, and a pack of anti-nausea medication. As she walked towards the kitchen, Zach smiled to himself, taking comfort in what he had just witnessed. Not only was Halyn attractive, smart, and irresistible, she was also selfless, accepting, and an honest caregiver. He had never been taken care of in this way. At that moment, he knew Halyn was different from anyone he had ever dated previously, and it started to alarm him. He was never one to commit fully to a relationship before, but there was something different and genuine about Halyn from the moment he met her. No matter how hard he tried to shake how fast he was falling for her, he couldn't. She was always on his mind and the thought that she could be the one frightened him. Zach gathered enough energy to get himself up and out of bed after an excruciating few days of being sick. Halyn's presence was the only thing that kept him sane. Food poisoning was not something he wished on anyone. In hindsight, awareness of his diagnosis sooner would have been ideal because, in retrospect, he didn't have to avoid getting close to Halyn while she cared for him. He had avoided all physical contact with her in fear of getting her sick, and now he ached for her more than ever.

" Where are you going?" Eric asked as Zach grabbed his keys and headed for the front door.

" Sorry mom, I'm going to the store and to see my girlfriend. I'll be back by bedtime." Zach replied sarcastically.

"Going to see Halyn? "

" Yes. I need to do something for her. She took care of me all week and I need to repay her."

"You really like this girl don't you?"

"Yes. Why do you ask?"

" Oh I don't know, maybe the fact that you have been in bed or beside the toilet all week, and the first place you want to go now that you have resurrected is to see her. " Eric winked at him.

"I'll see you later." Zach left, with the door slamming behind him.

With a brisk jog, he made his way to his car, trying to come up with a creative way to surprise Halyn. He had no idea what he would have done without her this past week. He began pondering all of Halyn's likes, dislikes, hobbies, and interests. Suddenly he had an idea. It was Friday night and Halyn usually studied at the library on

Friday nights, since it was the quietest night of the week. She was not one for a crowd or attention. It was just one more of Halyn's adoring qualities. After parking his car at the entranceway of the library, he decided he would risk getting a ticket. He could barely see out the window for the short drive to the main campus. The library was desolate, with only the sound of photocopiers and the librarian restocking shelves. Surprisingly, Halyn's study nook was empty. Perplexed, he reached into his pocket to message her. " She said she would be here." Zach thought out loud.

" Well if it isn't the patient." Her voice echoed from behind him. It was mellow and angelic. Zach turned to face Halyn, She caressed a latte in both hands and was dressed in her joggers and a fitted sweatshirt. So simple, yet perfect.

" Well hello. You are just who I've been looking for." Zach pointed over to Halyn's study booth. "I thought you would be over there."

" I was, and then I needed a change of scenery. The sunset was breathtaking tonight before the rainclouds took over. And there we so many stars, too many to count

" There are millions of stars right in front of us, but I'd rather just look at you." He recited as he leaned in to kiss her forehead. Halyn blushed as she sipped her coffee.

" On that note, since you took such great care of me this week, I was hoping I could take you to dinner. Or better yet, make you dinner if you'd prefer a night in."

Halyn glanced over at her notes sprawled along the desk in front of her. " I guess this can wait. I usually don't put off my work, but I think I can make an exception for you."

" I like where this is going," Zach replied confidently.

" Should I meet you at your place in a few minutes?"

" I have a better idea. I will come to pick you up in an hour. You'll need to pack an overnight bag." He winked at Halyn. She was blatantly anxious. "Honestly, you won't be disappointed." He bellowed as he made his way back down the stairs of the library.

Rowan came bounding into Halyn's room as she was packing her last item and strategically folding it to fit in her modest duffle bag. She had packed a pair of pyjamas, toiletries, a hairdryer, and a change of clothes for the following day. Rowan was aghast at the items she witnessed going into the bag. " That will never do. You are going to your first sleepover with your boyfriend. You are still in the need to impress him stage of this relationship. You need to stretch the boundaries of your comfort zone a little. Here." Rowan tore out all of the items Halyn had meticulously placed in her bag and replaced them with other items from Halyn's closet, as well as some of her own belongings she had brought over.

"You also need options," Rowan exclaimed from

the closet. She shimmied her way through the pile of clothes on the floor that she had created in haste. " Here's another bag. You can put your toiletries, hairdryer, and my curling wand in here. Here's some red lipstick. Put that in your purse."

" Why do I need red lipstick?"

" All guys like a girl with red lipstick. And clothing that shows your curves. Here, put this in there too." She threw a push up bra and a laced tank top in Halyn's face. Halyn complied.

"Where are your hoop earrings?"

" Rowan, I understand that you are trying to help, but Zach and I are just going to have a quiet night in. I'm not going out! I've got a wardrobe for a trip to the Bahamas in here."

" Well at least make sure you have a matching bra and underwear set on."

" Rowan!"

" Ok I'll leave, but just remember the red lipstick when he shows up." Rowan placed a delicate kiss on her sister's cheek and clicked her way out the door in her thigh-high boots.

Halyn glanced at the clock. She had two minutes to spare. She contemplated what other items she might need. Aside from her belongings, she knew she needed to gather her thoughts and slow down her racing mind. Although she was excited at the potential of becoming an official couple this weekend, she wasn't able to push aside the impending nervousness she felt. This was entirely out of her comfort zone, but she was elated at the possibilities. After gathering her courage and composing herself, she made one last adjustment before making her way downstairs to meet Zach, who she was confident she would call her boyfriend by the end of the weekend.

She looked in the mirror and put on her red lipstick.

CHAPTER 7

Zach's eyes met Halyn's as she appeared from around the concrete pillar, at the entrance of her building. She absorbed his gaze and read the anticipation in his eyes. As she walked towards his car, Zach exited from the driver's side, rushing to the passenger side before she could open the door herself.

" My lady." He said as he waved her into the car.

" So where are we going?" She asked as she crouched slowly into the front passenger seat.

" Oh, I'm not going to make it that easy for you. I need to build up the excitement and keep you on your toes. " H slammed his door shut, turning on the ignition with a sly grin on his face.

" Uggggh!" Halyn exclaimed. " I don't like surprises."

" Well, this time you don't have much of a choice. I suggest enjoying the scenery. We'll be in the car for about an hour."

Zach glanced down at Halyn's hand that was resting on her purse. He reached over slowly and intertwined his fingers in hers for the hour-long drive. It was completely dark outside when

Zach and Halyn approached their destination. Despite studying her surroundings throughout the drive, she was unfamiliar with the areas outside of Dryden. All she could conclude was that they were in the mountains and away from most of civilized society. She could feel the increasing altitude for the latter part of their drive. Her ears popped as she looked outside her window at the first sight of a lit-up building in the distance. Zach turned a corner and drove slowly down a narrow road, towards the light. As they came closer to it, Halyn was able to make out the outline of a small log cabin, tucked away behind hundreds of trees, a healthy distance away from the road. It was quaint, like out of a storybook, with smooth mahogany wooden logs stacked perfectly parallel to each other. An intricate archway flanked the entrance where lanterns lit up the stairs leading into the charming interior of the cabin. Wooden beams lined the ceiling from one length of the structure to the other. A floor to ceiling cobblestone fireplace, the centerpiece of the cabin, was lit with crackling flames, illuminating a sofa and an open bottle of champagne and chocolate-covered strawberries on a glass table directly in front of it.

" Go ahead inside." Zach smiled at Halyn and kissed her cheek, releasing her hand as she walked towards the fireplace.

    Halyn was speechless as she approached the sofa. It was draped with rose petals and a pair of soft fur blankets. She was unable to find intelligible words until Zach broke the lasting silence between them. " Do you like it?" He asked, trying to read her expression. He wasn't able to tell if she was delighted or depressed in the moment. His heart was in his throat as he waited in anticipation for her response." Halyn?" He asked again.

" I love it." She said softly as she gracefully pulled Zach over the back of the couch and onto the blankets in front of the fire. It was warm and the heat from both the fire and Zach's kiss seemed to relax Halyn's anxious mind instantly. " How on earth did you have time to plan all of this today?" She asked as they both came up for air.

" I know the owner. So I called her up and she came right over and set it up for me. The rose petals were an extra touch. I didn't ask for that." He laughed as he threw a handful of the petals in Halyn's face.

" Shall we?" Halyn asked, eyeing up the bottle of champagne within reach.

"After you." He motioned Halyn towards the fire.

After two glasses of champagne, Zach and Halyn lay intertwined on the sofa with power ballads softly echoing off the cathedral ceiling. Both of them sat in silence for a few moments. Halyn's mind was calm and at the same time, Zach's was racing.

" What's wrong?" Halyn asked as she read Zach's distant eyes. " Hey!" She snapped her fingers, breaking his fixed gaze on the fire. "Earth to Zach!"

"Yo!" he exclaimed escaping from his racing thoughts.

"I asked if something was wrong."

Zach let out an exasperated sigh. "No. Nothing is wrong. Quite the opposite actually."

"How so?" Halyn asked as she moved in closer to Zach's shirtless chest, taking note of his perfectly formed abdominals.

"I've just never felt this way with anyone before. I find myself consumed with thoughts of you all day every day. I want to spend all of my time with you, and everything has just been so perfect so far. Too perfect."

"Too perfect? How can any of this be too perfect?"

"I don't know, like too good to be true. I can't find a single fault in you."

"Isn't that a good thing?" Halyn asked as she took another sip of champagne, her cheeks feeling flush.

"I guess, I just like you a lot and don't want to be disappointed in the future."

"Future? I thought we were taking this one day at a time?" Halyn asked honestly.

"Is that what you still want? I ask because I can certainly see you in my future. I've been thinking about it a lot lately. I would love it if you would be my girlfriend."

Halyn attempted to hide her excitement

but to no avail. She jumped onto Zach, her hair in his face and planted a kiss on his shoulder, and then his neck and back to his lips, where they stayed until the early hours in the morning.

  Zach awoke as the sun rose through the rustic windows, to the sight of their clothes scattered on the floor throughout the room. Luckily, he was able to function on virtually no sleep. He slowly moved his leg off Halyn, in an attempt not to wake her. She stirred for a moment. He paused. As she fell back into a deep sleep, he quietly made his way to the kitchen to brew a pot of coffee. As its aroma filled the air, he watched Halyn, his girlfriend, sleeping, her chest rising a descending peacefully. She was angelic and beautiful even in sleep. They had experienced a pivotal night together, a huge step forward in their relationship, and planning their future together, a moment Zach had never genuinely experienced before or expected.

CHAPTER 8

As the first snowflakes of the year fell on Dryden College's cobblestone walkways, Zach and Eric were making their way to the Grand Hall for their last exam before Christmas break. The oak trees that once donned brightly coloured leaves at the start of the school year were now decorated in periwinkle twinkle lights. Zach pulled his collar up above his chin as he made his way through a wind tunnel and under a disappointingly littered bridge. Staring off into space, Zach was thinking about Halyn and the months they had just spent together. They were clearly an item, but neither of them had initiated or used the word "Love" yet. Zach had been playing it slow for two reasons. One, Halyn had been fairly adamant from the beginning that she had just ended a relationship and didn't want anything serious. Two, Zach was battling his intense feelings for her. He had never fallen so fast for anyone and this caused many sleepless nights since their cabin in the woods adventure. And it was a conversation that he wasn't ready to have with Halyn since he couldn't understand it himself.

Eric could see that something was on Zach's mind, but he wasn't one for intimate conversations. He stayed quiet for a moment, analyzing his friend's demeanour. Reluctantly, Eric decided to bite the bullet.

"What's going on in that head of yours?"

"I really like her Eric." He Paused. "I really really like her."

"Ok dude. That's what you said about your ex too."

"But Halyn is different, and it's terrifying. What if she's the one? I'm not ready for that and it's only been a few months. I want to be with her all the time. I miss her when I'm not with her. Every corny love song I hear and every show I watch makes me think of her. She's so good to me too, too good in fact. I don't deserve someone like that. I'm terrified of commitment and she's getting more invested every day. Maybe even more than I am."

"Ahhh how the tables have turned," Eric said

"What do you mean?"

"Well, she wasn't exactly begging for you to like her at the beginning. I specifically remember her staring at you with daggers in her eyes a few months ago. Now, you're the one who is conflicted."

"I'm not conflicted about my feelings for her. The problem is that I'm too sure."

Zach sat down at his assigned desk just in time with only two black pens in hand. As the exam timer began, he peered two rows over to see

Halyn deeply engrossed in her essay. If a pen could catch on fire, hers would have. He admired her work ethic, her self-awareness, and her ability to not give a crap what anyone thought of her type-A personality. She owned herself in a quietly confident and humble way.

Halyn caught his glance and winked at him. He still had butterflies every time he saw her, a sense of attraction that he couldn't explain. He hated that he was so unsure and insecure about where their relationship stood. He couldn't deny his overpowering feelings towards her, but he also couldn't shake the anxiety he felt when he thought about the commitment that would come with them being exclusive. He couldn't help but remember his parents and their troubled relationship and how much it had likely affected his own psyche, afraid of repeating the offense himself. Halyn deserved better, someone who could reciprocate the level of commitment she was giving him, but he also couldn't bear the thought of her being with anyone else. When the timer rang at the end of the exam, Zach stood up, grabbed his pens, and walked out the door of the crowded hall, without saying a word to Halyn.

      Two rows over, Halyn sat in her seat watching Zach purposefully dash towards the door. She continued to sit at her desk as the other students chaotically made their way out of the exam room. A minute ago she was happy with how her exam went, but now she felt empty and gutted with disappointment that something was wrong with Zach. Usually, he was the first to greet her after a test or exam. Once the other students had cleared the exam hall, Halyn fled after him trying to trace his footsteps as tears welled up in her eyes. She felt a pang of disappointment and her gut was telling her that something wasn't right. His abrupt exit was blindsiding. "This was not how I planned to start my holidays." She said as she caught up with Rowan, Lucy, and Becca. After the exam, she had planned to go home and bake some Christmas cookies for Zach to take home to his family, a small, but thoughtful gesture for a family that she hadn't met yet. She was left disappointed when she was looking out the floor to ceiling, pane glass windows unable to find him. His car was no longer in the parking lot, confirming her fear that it wasn't the exam troubling him since he always offered her a ride home. Lucy, Becca, and Rowan startled her as she turned to walk back towards the Grand Hall to gather her belongings.

"What's wrong? Asked Becca. "You look like you just saw a ghost."

"Something is wrong," Halyn replied hesitantly.

"With what?" asked Lucy

"With Zach. He just left without even talking to me or offering me a ride home. It's so unlike him and I feel like it has to do with me and not the exam."

"Typical guy." retorted Rowan. Halyn gave

Rowan some serious side-eye.

"What? He's a typical guy running away when things get too serious. They all do it."

Lucy nudged Rowan with her elbow as Halyn's head dropped into her hands. "Look, you just need to talk to him. You can't be certain of what's going on and maybe its nothing to worry about. He likes you. It's pretty obvious"

"That's part of the problem though. He's LIKED me for a long time now. I think I might love him. But he hasn't even hinted at it himself. I'm getting seriously discouraged."

" You are overthinking this. Why don't you ask him?" Becca suggested.

Halyn was at a loss for words. It wasn't a bad idea. Maybe it was time for the talk that they had been avoiding. They had already gone on many dates and they texted each other all day, every day. When she wasn't spending the night with him, every morning she would wake up to a text reading " *Good morning Beautiful.*" He was the first person she thought of upon waking in the morning, and the last person she thought of before falling asleep at night. Halyn decided that she would meet up with Zach that night to discuss where their relationship was going and to see where his head was at during the exam today.

The following Saturday morning, Halyn had originally planned to do some Christmas shopping before heading back home for the holidays. Classes were finished for the semester, which meant all Halyn would have to worry about for the next two weeks was whether or not crazy Uncle Ted was coming to dinner with his two spoiled daughters who would surely end up stealing something or tormenting her and Rowan. Christmas was always a circus in the Curtis household. Halyn and Rowan came from a large family and a very eclectic one. And although general conversation was minimal, there was always someone who couldn't refrain from the personal inquiries about their love lives, something Halyn was fiercely private about on a good day. So naturally, family functions were entertaining, to say the least.

Halyn opened her eyes to see her retro alarm clock reading 7:00 AM. Normally, she was not an early riser, but she hadn't been able to fall back asleep. It had been a full seventy-two hours since she had seen or heard from Zach. He had never returned her texts after the exam and wasn't home when she decided to stop by, which meant that she did not have the opportunity to meet with him. With her mind beginning to spin again, she quickly stood out of bed and walked towards her desk. Ellie was still asleep and Halyn did not want to wake her since she was up talking to her boyfriend all night. She tiptoed back into bed after retrieving her phone. No "*Good Morning Beautiful!*" text. Halyn felt sick and even though she was lying down again, she felt clammy and dizzy.

He wasn't returning her messages. In her mind, the worst part of any situation was the unknown and she couldn't motivate herself to get out of bed for the rest of the morning.

Knock Knock Knock!

A pounding at the door startled Halyn. She sluggishly made her way into a seated position. Wearily gathering herself, she put on her slippers and stood up. The room was still spinning, but she started towards the door that was continuing to vibrate.

"Knock Knock Knock!

"I'm coming. I'm coming," she whispered loudly, annoyed by the unwanted visitor's lack of patience. She opened the door still in her pyjamas, her hair in an unkempt bun and dark circles flanked her under eyes.

" What on earth happened to you?" Rowan was shocked to see her sister in her dishevelled state at two o'clock in the afternoon. "The only time I've ever witnessed you like this much of a hot mess was when we had food poisoning after that cruise a few years ago. What's going on?"

" I just woke up. I always look like this when I wake up. I was up late and it's cold out, so I thought I would stay in bed a while longer."

" He hasn't gotten back to you has he?"

" No. He's probably busy packing to go back home for the break."

Rowan tilted her head sideways and shot her sister a disappointed glance. "You and I both know what you need. We need a girl gang day out to get you through this. What did you want to do today?"

" I was planning to start my shopping. But, I'm not so sure I want to do that now. I'd rather stay in bed until Zach messages me back."

" He may not get back to you today. You need a day out with your sister and your friends and I'm not taking no for an answer. You need your relationship fairies to knock some sense into you, at the mall, full disclosure and you need to also drown your worries in ice cream. "

Halyn caught a glance of herself in the mirror. Disappointed in her reflection, she knew Rowan was right again. She needed to figure out how she was going to approach Zach. It was one thing to be upset with her or to even be doubtful about their relationship, but it was another thing for him to ignore her altogether. It was just plain disrespectful.

As Halyn pulled herself together to go on a shopping outing with Lucy, Becca, and Rowan, she saw Zach's favourite T-shirt in the closet and put it on. He loved it when she wore a plain fitted T-shirt with skinny jeans. It was simple, yet stylish and complimented his style as well. She put on the earrings that he had just bought her on a recent date, threw on some mascara, brushed her teeth, and followed Rowan to Lucy and Becca's dorm. They were already waiting outside for her, all decked out in statement outfits.

When they arrived at the mall, the hustle and bustle of the holiday season was in full force. Christmas music was playing in every store, crowds of people gathered around the hottest holiday wish list items and Halyn quickly observed that they would need to be prepared for long line ups at the registers. Each store was decorated with mistletoe and twinkle lights. Halyn managed to muster up a slight smile when she noticed a dancing Santa Claus in a store window, shaking his hips side to side.

"What's first? Shopping or ice cream?" asked Lucy. They all looked in Halyn's direction.

" I guess ice cream," Halyn replied feeling as though she were being interrogated.

As they made their way through the crowds, the girls didn't hesitate to bring up Zach. The line up was long in the ice cream parlour, which was surprising to Halyn since it was winter.

"Has he messaged you back yet?" asked Lucy.

Halyn reached into the pocket of her jeans and pulled out her phone. She scrolled through the few unanswered texts that she had received from her parents. There were no messages from Zach. "No, nothing yet."

"What if you sent him a message simply saying that you are concerned that something may have happened to him? If he's a decent human, he'd likely message you back so you wouldn't have to worry anymore." Lucy made a good point, and she was concerned about him. She had run so many scenarios in her mind over the last couple of days.

"Maybe he lost his phone." Replied Becca.

" He would have come to my dorm to tell me that."

"Or, he is somewhere out of range for service to his phone."

" He would have told me he was going out of town."

" Maybe he's just a jerk and has decided that now that he has you, he needs to start the chase with someone else. I'll take the cookies and cream please, " Rowan replied as she ordered her ice cream without batting an eye.

"You are unbelievable Rowan. Why do you have to be so insensitive?"

The ice cream server stared at them with an awkward look on his face, waiting for Halyn to order hers. Lucy and Becca decided to wait outside the store for the sisters since they didn't want to get involved in their sibling squabble.

" I'm not insensitive, I'm just being real."

"Well sometimes, people need you to be less real and more supportive. You don't think I already know that he might be uninterested now? It's like rubbing salt in the wound Rowan and that's the last thing I need. I need help working through this, but instead you........"

"Halyn!" Lucy and Becca ran over to her, startled, and unable to find their words.

" Ummm." Lucy looked at Becca and they both

turned towards her, swallowing their ice cream hastily without enjoyment.

"What?" asked Halyn hesitantly.

"He's here," Becca whispered.

Halyn's eyes widened as she looked past Becca's shoulder. In the distance, she could see Zach's tall, athletic physique, his back turned towards them. He obviously hadn't seen Lucy and Becca outside the ice cream parlour and he appeared to be waiting for someone as he read the back cover of a magazine. Halyn hustled the girls around the corner so that they could spy on him from behind a wall without getting noticed. Something seemed off and Halyn had an unsettled feeling in her stomach. Suddenly, she wasn't hungry for ice cream anymore. They waited behind the wall for what seemed like an eternity before Zach turned towards them. They quickly hid behind the wall in sequence, taking large breaths as the server at the ice cream parlour watched them inquisitively.

"Well, he seems to be feeling just fine." Halyn, quipped, frustrated even more so than before.

" Who do you think he's waiting for?" asked Becca.

"Probably Eric," Halyn replied confidently.

Halyn's confidence quickly turned into disbelief when she turned the corner again. Beside Zach, in all her glory, was Marissa Jacobs. He was smiling at her and she gave him a flirtatious hug. Halyn's worst nightmare was coming true when she soon realized that Marissa was the one Zach was waiting for. He had gone to the mall with her. Marissa of all people was on a date with Zach.

" That slithery bitch," yelled Rowan.

"SHHHHHHH!" the others all replied in unison. None of the girls could speak in this spiralling moment as they watched Marissa flirt with Zach and finally rest her head on his shoulder while wrapping her arm around his waist.

"This is a nightmare. I can't watch anymore." Halyn fled the ice cream parlour, past Zach and Marissa, and ran down the escalator. Zach caught a glimpse of her in his periphery and started towards her. By the look in his eye, he knew he was in trouble.

" Don't you dare go near her right now!" Rowan yelled, stopping him directly in his path, her trembling hand in his face. Marissa stood behind him, grinning from ear to ear, confidently rubbing salt in the wound. She had won.

CHAPTER 9

Halyn spent the summer replaying her relationship with Zach over and over again in her mind. She never received any messages from him other than to turn down her offers to meet up and talk. She assumed he perceived them as her wanting to get back together based on his one and only reply. "I'm over it and you should be too," was the last sentence he wrote in his single text. It was like a dagger straight to the heart, and a presumptuous one at that. He never officially broke up with her, not even with a brief phone call.

Overthinking consumed her and she was unable to understand how he could just drop her out of thin air. It was as if their relationship had never existed and everything that they had experienced together was insignificant. Insignificance was a strong feeling and it was leading to an overpowering emotional mess. Once a girl with a quiet confidence, she now had trouble mustering up her self worth. On several occasions, she tried to find some kind of explanation as to what she may have done to deserve Zach's harsh exit from their relationship. Each time, through her hours of tears, she was never able to think of a single event or conversation that would warrant the level of disrespect she was continuing to receive. Even though she knew she could never be with someone who treated her so deplorably, she couldn't help but feel a steady, undeniable attraction to him. Her head and her heart were in two completely different places and she hated it. She despised what he did to her, but still loved him at the same time, and even though they had never spoken those three palpable words, she began to realize that she did in fact, love Zach Payne after all. Halyn and Zach had a natural connection, one in which she had never had with anyone else. She was free to be real and open with him about anything and everything. They shared intimate conversations and Halyn laid her heart on her sleeve for him, something she was never comfortable nor motivated to do in past relationships. It was easy and organic with Zach, a relationship for the movies or storybooks and she was confident they had the potential to be incredible together.

    To Halyn, the foundation of a good relationship was based on honesty, trust, a natural connection, and respect. All but one of those were now gone. Her heart had been shattered by the one who pursued her. He reeled her in like a fish and she took the bait. And no matter how often or hard she tried to fight her surface-level feelings towards him, which was all she could feel at this point, she couldn't get over the nightmare of harsh, unforeseeable rejection. She couldn't deny the way she felt when he walked into a room, his smile, or his soft and caring presence. How was that all gone now? How could someone who took so much of her heart just be gone in an instant, no explanation, and no regard for her feelings?

She, lay in the hammock in the back yard of her parents' home having eaten nothing but a piece of toast and a handful of grapes all day. She was dreading going back to school the next day and having to see Zach. She had purposely picked classes that he would not be in, making sure that she was still aligned with all of the subjects she needed for medical school. Zach dreaded chemistry and Marissa didn't have the grades to move forward with medical school. Rowan had heard earlier in the summer that Marissa had dropped out of their program, which wasn't surprising to anyone. She had also learned that Zach and Marissa were dating and rumour had it, he was spending a lot of time at her lake house and decided to head back to Dryden two weeks early to stay with her there. The idea of Zach staying at Marissa's lake house made Halyn cringe since it was where she and Zach always said they officially started dating. Waves of jealousy and rage flowed through her body like a never-ending pendulum. Daily, the abundance of cynical self-talk consumed her when she thought about how she couldn't measure up to Marissa and that it made perfect sense as to why Zach would choose her. Marissa was a stylish, tall, and fit goddess who stood about 5'10, fake perky breasts and all while sitting on a pile of money. What man wouldn't want that? The superficial junk she could understand, but her character and, need to be the loudest in the room personality is what Halyn was unable to get past.

" Halyn, it's time to come in for dinner!" Rowan shouted from the patio door, waking her from her daydream.

"I'm coming." She remained on the hammock, under the sun for another 5 minutes before she heard another holler.

"It's your favourite dinner. We couldn't disappoint the birthday girl." Her mother shouted across the yard with excitement.

September 2nd was Halyn and Rowan's birthday, and although she was not in the mood to celebrate, Halyn couldn't disappoint her mother who always made family birthdays out to be momentous occasions. Even though they had reached adulthood, they always had cake, birthday hats, and friends would pop over to surprise them. Her mom would always try to keep it a secret, but after 20 years, they knew exactly what to expect. Halyn rolled out of the hammock, put on her flip-flops, and sunhat. She stretched towards the sun, breathing in the crisp air. Half asleep, she made her way along the stone path of the back yard, up the quaint patio and into the kitchen. Just as she suspected, she found Lucy, Becca, and Rowan all seated around the dining room table.

" SURPRISE! They all shouted as she walked in. Halyn smiled, grateful that the girls had taken the time out of their day to make the trip to her family home to celebrate, even though school was starting up again the following morning.

She smiled graciously. " Thanks for coming. Mom you didn't have to do all of this," she said. "And how come it wasn't a surprise for Rowan?" she asked.

"We thought you could use the pick me up. So I helped get the girls here for a fun girl's night." Rowan chimed in, proud of her humanitarianism.

" So no cake, balloons, or party hats?" Halyn looked around, noticing these items were absent. Typically, her mother would have streamers and balloons running from corner to corner on the ceiling. But there were no decorations.

"Oh, there will be cake." Her mother replied, insulted that her daughters would even ask.

" Mom wouldn't let us get away without it," Rowan whispered behind her hand in Halyn's direction. "But, after cake, we are headed to the spa!"

Halyn took her seat at the dining room table with little expression on her face. The girls immediately knew that Halyn wasn't keen on leaving the house.

"Halyn, you have been cooped up in this house all summer. A spa is a place where you can relax, get pampered, and hang out with your closest friends without anyone else around. We can talk and get you looking fab and fresh for the first day of school. That jerk's jaw will drop when he sees you tomorrow." Rowan continued.

" At least the first part of that sounded enticing." Halyn snapped back.

"I still have so much packing to do and I was hoping to get the course outlines read before we start tomorrow". The girls all paused, staring in Halyn's direction. Lucy chimed in, asking Halyn exactly what the other girls were thinking.

"Who pre-reads the course outlines while still on summer break? We need to get you out that door and into the spa before your brain explodes. Do they have a spa treatment for brainiacs?" asked Rowan, laughing at her own joke.

Halyn reluctantly gave in and accompanied the girls to the day spa. When they arrived, Halyn five senses were awakened with the oasis that was surrounding her. The music was inviting and the décor feminine. White plush loungers and couches filled the waiting area, with pink and rose gold accents surrounding the room. The spa was lit up by soft white ambient lighting that set the mood for a calm evening ahead. Accompanying the fruit infused water station were 4 robes rolled intricately with their names strategically placed in gold calligraphy on pink scented paper. The spa smelled of eucalyptus and lavender. The girls sat down on the plush couches after donning their robes and were greeted by a middle-aged lady who looked like she was ready for one of those 90's glamour shots, perm and all. She smelled of strong perfume but had a warm, friendly presence. She approached them with a tray of champagne, one of which was significantly larger than the rest.

" Who is the guest of honour?" the 90's glam queen asked.

Halyn timidly lifted her hand, eyeing the tall glass of champagne. The lady reached to the side of her tray and placed a pink rock candy stick in Halyn's champagne. The drink fizzed unexpectedly and the girls simultaneously applauded. She handed the drink to Halyn and smiled. "I'm Natasha, please enjoy your spa experience."

" Let's get this party started!" Exclaimed Rowan.

" Where to first?" asked Lucy

" You will be starting with pedicures in the luxury nail suite. Follow me." Natasha answered without missing a beat. She waved the four girls towards her, leading them down a hall that was draped with waterfalls running down the walls. Halyn was impressed with the attention to detail that each room offered as she weaved throughout the spa, all while drinking her champagne in record time. It was both delicious and relaxing. She felt an instant warmth throughout her body as she sat down on the heated massage chair awaiting her.

"This is the most relaxing way to finish a summer break. Great idea Rowan!" Becca declared without looking away from her champagne glass.

"I'd be pretty relaxed too if I drank that huge glass of champagne in less than two minutes." Replied Lucy. The girls all laughed looking over at Halyn who had a guilty expression on her face.

"Then I have to say, it's a good time to bring up Barbie and Ken and discuss how we are going to help Halyn navigate them tomorrow." Said Rowan.

" Has he called to wish you a happy birthday?" asked Becca.

"No. I haven't heard from him in weeks. He never really answered any of my messages other than to simply tell me that he's too busy to meet with me."

" So you're saying that he never even officially broke up with you?"

" No explanation, no phone call, no replies to any of my messages, nothing."

" The girls all took a sip of their champagne, in shock with what they were hearing."

" Why didn't you tell us all of this?" Asked Becca

" I don't know. I guess I didn't want to ruin everyone's summer with my depressing love life. Or lack thereof."

" I don't understand it," said Lucy angrily. " He was so into you. It's all he ever talked about. And he wanted so badly for me to hook the two of you up. I genuinely thought he was a better guy than that. I don't think any of us saw this coming."

"What I would do to get into that peanut-sized

brain of his." Rowan retorted, full of animosity.

" Me too. Trust me." Halyn chose her nail color and immersed her feet into the warm water under her chair. "Thanks for bringing me here. I needed this more than I thought. I wasn't sure I would sleep tonight, but this might just do the trick."

" What's the plan for going back tomorrow? Do you want to come with us?" asked Lucy, pointing at Becca.

" Honestly, I will be fine. Rowan and I are going to go to campus early in the morning before everyone else gets there. I plan to spend the day organizing my room and getting some groceries."

"Don't forget to read those course outlines." Rowan snapped back.

Halyn sent her a glare, but with a smile on the corner of her mouth. "Touche."

" What are you going to say to Zach when you see him?" Asked Becca.

" I don't know. I'm hoping to talk to him before I see him. I'd like to sit down and have a conversation and get everything off of my chest so that we can move past all of this and move on with our lives. Well, I can at least move on with my life. He evidently already has."

" Is that really what you want?" Asked Rowan as she tapped her nails against the armrest of the chair.

" To move on? Yes, I think so."

"So there is no shred of your being that still has feelings for him? Asked Lucy honestly.

"Look, am I still attracted to him? Yes. Will I get butterflies when I see him? Yes. That doesn't just go away. But, the thought of dating him nauseates me. I can't imagine ever being with someone who one day is planning our future, and then the next, proceeds about his day like I don't even exist. I need someone I can trust, and who will be honest with me no matter how much it hurts. I just don't see him as my person anymore. We had an amazing few months together, better than I could have ever imagined. Our connection was solid and real. But that is all gone, and it's now a rip in my soul that I don't think can ever be mended. I don't know what he could ever say to make me understand it all, which is why I hate that my heart still aches for him when I see him in a picture or a dream. My heart and my head are in two exhaustively different places.

    The girls sat in silence for a few minutes as they absorbed Halyn's heartbroken monologue until Rowan finally broke the silence as Natasha sauntered back into the room. "She'll have another champagne."

    The next morning, Halyn woke up to the sound of birds chirping outside her bedroom window and pounding in her temples. It was still dark outside and she could hear the humming of the early morning traffic. It was going to be a long day. Although her thoughts of Zach had consumed her mind for weeks, she was still looking forward to getting back into a school routine. She could smell the scent of freshly printed books already and couldn't wait to get back to her favourite nook in the library. She gathered her luggage and placed her course outlines and highlighters in her purse before taking one last glance at the room she grew up in. Through the foyer window, she could see Rowan packing up the trunk of the car, multiple suitcases still on the ground. "Is there going to be any room for my bags?" She thought to herself. After packing the car up to the roof and even having to sit cross-legged due to bags under her feet, Halyn took a large sip of her coffee and rolled down the window. The girls waved to their parents and set off in their own second-hand car, which felt like a luxury to have on campus this year.

" Isn't this awesome?" We have a car this year!" Rowan couldn't contain the excitement. " Maybe we can almost run over you know who like he did to you last year on the first day?"

" Actually, I was hoping we could not mention or discuss Zach because I want to enjoy the scenic ride and the first day back to campus. I need to focus on the path ahead to medical school. I'm sincerely looking forward to getting back to Dryden otherwise."

" Fair enough. Although I think you may be the only person I know that is truly excited for school and not just for the social aspect. I wonder if there will be some new guys in our classes?"

Rowan drank far too much coffee, so after four hours due to three bathroom breaks and a speeding ticket, the girls pulled up to the campus. There were already swarms of new students and their parents blocking many of the entrances. Furniture and luggage surrounded the gardens and masses of vehicles lined the roadways.

"I thought we were getting here early to beat the crowds."

"Joke's on us." Replied Rowan. After they parked the car in their designated spot, they started unpacking under the warm September sun until they heard a familiar high-pitched voice.

" Hi, Halyn and Rowan. How was your summer?" Halyn turned to see Ellie greeting her with open arms. Halyn smiled and hugged her roommate who she was relieved to see. The familiarity of Ellie was comforting.

" It was relaxing thank you." She lied as she changed the subject. "Where are all your bags?"

"Oh, I am living off-campus this year." Ellie pointed in the direction of the entrance to campus.

" I see." Halyn felt a pang of anxiety in her chest but put on a brave smile for her friend. " I guess I will have a new roommate this year?" She asked, even though she already knew the answer.

" I guess so." Ellie winked at Rowan who proceeded to smile and peek at Halyn's expressionless face.

"I hope you have a great year. I'm living with my boyfriend now."

Halyn felt a surge of jealousy. She had hoped she and Zach would be living together at some point in the coming months. That was what he had suggested the day before he figuratively pushed her off a cliff. "That's exciting for both of you. Congratulations." Halyn responded honestly and reached out to hug her friend. Even though she was envious, she was happy for Ellie.

"Thanks. Well, I guess I will bump into you around campus. Certainly I will see you in the library soon."

Halyn waved to Ellie as she walked away towards her boyfriend who greeted Halyn with a friendly wave. She waved back and then swiftly turned towards her sister. "What was that all about?" she asked. "Did you know I was going to have a new roommate? Because it sure looked like it."

Rowan gave her a caring glance and clasped her hands in Halyn's. "I wanted to keep this a surprise for a bit longer, but, Mom and Dad are paying for us to stay in the Guildwood Residence this year." Rowan's face was beaming in anticipation of her sister's reaction. Halyn suddenly felt a glimmer of hope. "You, me, Lucy, and Becca are all rooming together this year."

"Really? No way! It's not a joke, right? This is amazing!" she replied as she remembered when

Zach pointed out the residence to her last year.

Rowan smiled. It was the first time she had seen her sister truly smile all summer. "Well, let's go!" Rowan seized Halyn's hand and they ran towards their new residence, excited to see that only a handful of people had already arrived.

Guildwood was a stark contrast to the massive, dorm she lived in last year. It was a quaint and secluded, abutting the city's only lake. So naturally, it came with a higher price tag. Not that Halyn felt the need to live in the nicest residence on campus, but she also wasn't going to complain either since the opportunity came knocking. Inside the contemporary building's front doors were marble pillars varnished with detailing similar to the European gothic era. A large elegant staircase engulfed the middle of the room and was the showpiece of the structure. The girls headed up the staircase where they received the keys to their apartment on the top floor.

When they opened the detailed, hand-crafted wooden door, they were overwhelmed by the view overlooking the gardens and the lake to the south. In their minds, they likely had the most desired apartment on campus. Halyn immediately went to her bedroom. It was spacious and had its own bathroom. She was simply pleased to have her own space and not be woken up to the sound of clicking on a keyboard at 3 AM when Ellie would have her late-night, online conversations. She tolerated Ellie just fine, but it was certainly better to have her own private space. She immediately took out her pens and paper and started drawing out a floor plan for her room, envisioning a corner desk facing the window that looked out onto the lake. This was her haven.

Halyn's thoughts were interrupted by the sound of heavy keys clinking outside her door. She left her room reluctantly but was happy to see Becca and Lucy blunder through the door, hollering at the top of their lungs in a frenzy.

" How cool is this? Look at that spectacular view!" exclaimed Becca

Lucy came over to hug Halyn. " What do you think? Were you surprised?"

" I honestly can't believe this. I think I'm still in shock and thank you for the room with the large windows. It is perfect." Halyn replied appreciatively.

" We are going to have so much damn fun here." Yelled Rowan. Let's unpack the car, and put on some music!" she suggested as she did a little jig around the room.

"I'm so happy. What would I do without you all? You're good for my soul." Halyn's eyes lit up as she paused to appreciate the moment and her friends who had gone out of their way to make Halyn's experience at school, post-non-breakup, more tolerable.

" Lucy, you find some tunes. We will be right back." Rowan ordered Lucy towards the radio, while she led Halyn out the door.

The sisters were on cloud nine as they dashed down the hallway, zig-zagging around other students. Halyn could never have imagined living in such a magnificent place on campus. Last year, she was fortunate to eat three meals a day on her budget. Now, she felt as though she was living in luxury. It was no lake house, like Zach's new home, but it was ideal for her and she was grateful for the opportunity.

As Halyn was daydreaming about all the events that would take place in their new apartment, she tripped on the bottom step of the grand staircase and fell face-first into the arms another student. With her head still down and humiliated, she gripped his arms to stop herself from falling to the ground. Once she found her equilibrium, she immediately recognized the soft skin and defined biceps that she was unable to let go of. They were Zach's arms. For a moment she was unable to look up, in fear that he would let her fall to the floor when he realized it was her. Finally, she came to her senses and slowly looked up into his crystal clear eyes. Butterflies filled her stomach and she struggled to take a full breath. She was in Zach's arms again. Suddenly mortified, she pushed him away, picked up her key from the floor, and started towards the door in a fury. Zach was at a loss for words. He watched her walk out the entrance and made a hasty decision to follow her to the parking lot. Halyn's embarrassment abruptly turned into rage when she realized what had happened.

"He should have just moved out of the way." She shouted

"Keep your cool. He's right behind us." Rowan rushed after Halyn.

"What do you mean he's right behind us? Is he following me? How dare he?" Halyn looked over her shoulder and gasped. She turned and stopped Zach in his tracks, anger, and resentment boiling in her blood. Her legs felt as though they could give out on her at any moment.

"I don't want you to take one step closer to me unless you are willing to talk, apologize, or both."

Zach looked at her with pain in his eyes. He had never seen this side of Halyn before, and honestly, he never thought he would. He knew her as gentle, sweet, and passive, someone who could calm him with just one beholding gaze. "I did this to her." He thought to himself. "I'll talk." He replied as he watched Rowan pull out their bags from the car. He tried to help her lift a heavy suitcase, but she shook her head in anger. He gracefully stepped back, maintaining a safe boundary.

"I'll take these bags up to the apartment and come back down in a few minutes. Call me if you need me." Rowan didn't take her eyes off of Zach as she walked away. Zach could feel Rowan's eyes on him, like daggers to his soul.

"Want to sit in my car?" He asked Halyn

"No, I certainly do not!" Halyn shouted, annoyed

at the question.

"Where would you like to talk?"

"Right here."

Zach looked around at the swarms of people surrounding them and pushed the overwhelming lack of privacy to the back of his mind.

"I don't even know where to start Zach. What's going on?"

"I think we should just be friends," Zach replied, unsure of what else to say. He was so taken aback by how Halyn had confronted him that he was unsure how to approach her question.

Halyn looked at Zach in astonishment, shaking her head and making a fist. "Is that honestly all you have to say?"

"I want you to know that I have thought a lot about everything. And I'm aware that I could be making the worst mistake of my life." He said honestly. "I was just really confused a few months ago and I didn't want to hurt you, but I don't know what else to say right now. I wasn't expecting to bump into you. Or catch you I guess."

"I can't believe this. So I'm not even worth a conversation or a return text? We had that amazing weekend together, you stumbled on your words when you accidentally said you loved me, and then days later, nothing. Like I didn't even exist. And all you have to say is that you want to be friends? I am a human being Zach with real feelings and you aren't acknowledging any of them!"

Zach stared at her blankly, frozen in one place, unable to speak. Halyn's posture sank when she realized he was not going to elaborate on his words. She walked away, depressed and hurt, with tears welling up her eyes. Zach watched her regretfully as the distance between them increased. Once she was out of sight, instead of following her, he went back up the grand staircase of Guildwood to Eric's new apartment. In that moment, he remembered how Halyn would call them the wolf pack, a solemn smile flashed across his face. The sound of Reggae filled the apartment as he walked in and it already smelled like a houseful of men, even though the guys had only been there for a couple of hours. Trudging slowly past the two first rooms, he noticed they were empty. Seconds later, the sound of a hammer hitting the wall of the master bedroom startled him and he made his way towards the racket. He was certain it was Eric. Without greeting his friend, Zach began to tell Eric about his recent encounter with Halyn.

" I'm such an idiot Eric. I don't know what I'm going to do having to see her all year at school. I don't know how to act around her. I hate that she hates me, and the worst part is, we probably have some classes together and how will either of us be able to focus in class with each other there?"

Eric stared at Zach, surprised by his friend's run-on sentence. Zach was breathing heavily. " Dude, it sounds like she is pretty mad. I would knock your ego down a couple of notches because she likely doesn't care now that you've gone and blown her off again. Eric started to swing the hammer, forcing Zach to take a few steps back. "Besides, you've got Marissa Jacobs now. You don't need to worry about any other girls at this point."

" I think I truly hurt her. You should have seen her. She was filled with rage, and she made a fist at me. I've never seen such serious cut-eye. I have never even seen Halyn angry before today." Zach shuddered as he came over to hold Eric's shelf. He was distinctly struggling to hang it.

" So talk to her then," Eric replied as if it were an easy answer.

"I can't."

"Why not?"

" Because I worry it may rekindle some old feelings and I can't get that caught up in her again. I think I loved her and that scares the hell out of me."

" Well do you love Marissa?' asked Eric as he put down the hammer and cracked open two beers.

" No, I don't. I've only been dating her for a few weeks. At least I don't think I do. Not yet anyway. I certainly don't feel the same way I did with Halyn."

Zach began to reminisce about his summer. He re-read Halyn's messages repeatedly, trying to find the right thing to say to her. He wanted to refrain from leading her on, but also didn't want her to think that he didn't care about her. So he simply chose not to reply to avoid the confrontation. He had put her on a pedestal of what a true girlfriend, lover, and potential wife could be, and that scared him off. He spent many hours conflicted with feeling both guilty for what he had done to Halyn, but also relieved that he was free of commitment. Following the exam back in December, Zach was on his way home when he ran into Marissa at the café. She asked him to come and sit next to her, as he was noticeably confused and vulnerable. After an hour and a half, Marissa had convinced him that Halyn wasn't the right person for him. With her piercing eyes and seductive smile, she gave him her manipulative relationship advice.

"The best way for a girl to deal is to not engage in conversation with them at all. She'll get over it faster that way. Plus, when the time is right, you need a woman, not a girl. I'm not looking for anything serious. But I can still give you a good time." She deceitfully advised him.

Marissa was reputable company. He enjoyed the attention he received by casually dating her and she was good arm candy. None of those attributes screamed commitment. He was able to experience her lavish lifestyle and surprisingly enjoyed the company of her family. Zach perceived Marissa as a confident woman who knew what she wanted, and he was somehow suddenly drawn to it. She let Zach drive the family's luxury cars and enjoyed feasts prepared by their household chef. On weekends, they went off to the Hamptons and made out on the beach daily. It wasn't until he moved into her lake house earlier when he realized he needed to let go of Halyn. She was still sending him messages and Marissa was becoming more annoyed with each ping of his phone.

While drinking his morning coffee on the deck, one humid summer morning, Marissa appeared in her lingerie, holding a cup of tea in one hand, and an object too small to make out, in the palm of her other hand. "I bought you a little gift." Marissa handed him a package that looked like it was wrapped in fourteen karat gold as she sipped her tea. Her eyes glared above the rim of the stone mug.

"Really? What's this for?" Zach adjusted his posture, and sat up comfortably on the chaise lounge, placing his coffee on the damp wooden deck below him.

Marissa, in only her silk robe, kissed him and sat on his lap facing him while leaving a stain of red lipstick across his mouth. "Just a little something I think you need." She said bewitchingly. Zach opened the box carefully. He could tell it was fragile. Inside the box was a new cell phone. One like he had never seen before.

"It's new. Not even out on the market yet." She said proudly.

"How did you get it?" he asked, his eyes as wide as a kid on Christmas morning.

"My daddy has some connections. So I made a few calls. Do you like it?"

"I love it. Let me get my SIM card from my other phone and put it in this one."

"Ah Ah Ah!" Marissa propelled Zach's body back onto his seat before he could fully stand up. "You don't need to. It has a new card and you have a new number. No more ex-girlfriends pestering you on the daily. I want you to be able to focus on us. I know it has been bothering you that she's been trying to talk incessantly. You don't need to worry about that anymore. I told her to back off."

Zach felt both relieved and guilty. But under her spell, he felt that Marissa was right. It was eating him up inside. He had been a coward and he was disappointed in how he handled the break-up, even though Marissa had been the Ringmaster. Halyn didn't deserve him. She deserved someone who could treat her like the queen she was. Selfishness and fear had consumed his neurotic thoughts and as things between the two of them became more serious, he realized that he was falling hard and wasn't ready for that level of commitment. Each time Zach read Halyn's messages, he could never capture the words to express how he was feeling. He thought it might just be easier to not say anything at all, as Marissa had suggested, and let time heal her wounds.

Marissa was a good distraction. He enjoyed her company and was certain that he could never feel the same way about her that he had felt for Halyn. He desired companionship, but not a commitment, at least not right now. A future with Halyn was a possibility, but with Marissa, he wasn't so sure. Lately, however, he was getting the impression that Marissa wanted more. At first, Marissa and Zach both settled on having some fun and liberal summer with no strings attached, but lately, Marissa was becoming more possessive about their time together. Zach knew that this most recent gift was less a gift for him, and more a tracking device for her. He predicted that she would boast about how her dad was able to get the newest phone on the market before anyone else, and it also gave her a way to keep him wrapped around her finger. He sat in the chaise lounge, Marissa on top of him, leaning in for a kiss. He couldn't resist her seductive request and they spent the rest of the night at her lake house making love under the stars with the waves crashing in on the beach behind them. How could he resist the lust and lifestyle that accompanied Marissa Jacobs? Any guy at Dryden would do anything to be in his shoes.

Zach awoke from his daydream" Do you want to go and grab some drinks at the lake house?" Zach asked Eric. " Marissa is expecting me home any minute. I promised her I'd be back before dinner. She has the chef making me his gourmet beer burgers. You can stay for dinner too."

" You have a curfew?" Eric let out a devious chuckle.

"It's not a curfew. We just made plans."

" Right. Last night you had to be back when the streetlights came on too." Eric replied sarcastically.

" Do you want to come to the lake house or not?"

" No. I'm going to stay here and finish getting the apartment set up. I'll see you in class in the morning."

"I can come and pick you up in Marissa's Benz tomorrow," Zach suggested

" Its ok dude, I can walk."

Zach was getting the feeling that Eric was throwing him some shade. Lately, Eric was distant and not answering some of his messages. Eric always had his face buried in his phone, so Zach knew he was getting them and today, he was feeling a separation of sorts with his best friend.

" Ok. I'll see you tomorrow." He replied, not wanting to ruffle any feathers. He had been through enough in the last hour. He pulled out his new phone, and his old one, just in case. No new messages.

CHAPTER 10

The first day of school was always one of Halyn's favourite days of the year, and although she was fairly confident she wasn't going to be in any of Zach or Marissa's classes, she still had a sneaking suspicion that she would have to endure running into them occasionally on campus. Based on yesterday's events, she was certain it was the first of many unwanted encounters with the pair. All summer, she had rehearsed a clever monologue for what she would say if she saw Zach again, but yesterday she wasn't prepared for her humiliating interaction. What was he doing at Guildwood anyway? He was living at Marissa's lake house as far as she knew and based on Zach's depiction of his parents, they would never pay for him to live there.

Halyn finished brushing her teeth and put on the new jean dress that Rowan gifted her on their birthday. With her hair slicked back in a ponytail and nothing but mascara on her face, she looked in the mirror and thought that maybe she could step up her fashion game. It was the first day of school after all. She needed to regain her confidence and really, she was always looking for an excuse to wear those fun dangly gold earrings she had tucked away in a shoebox under her bed for months. "Maybe it's also time to invest in a jewellery box," she thought to herself. She donned the earrings, picked up her books, and made her way to class.

The walk through campus was just as beautiful as last year, except this time, it came with a hint of nostalgia. She noticed new trees lining the median along the roadways and she was pleasantly surprised to see the school investing in the environment. She stopped when she came to the café and thought she would treat herself to a latte. She sighed at the sight of the long line up out the door and onto the wooden terrace. Despite the possibility of showing up a little late for class, it was the first day and they likely would not be covering any important material in the first ten minutes. Plus, she had already read the course outlines. Halyn texted Rowan, asking her to save a seat in class for her. After ordering lattes, she headed for the door glancing at her watch, optimistic she would make it to class on time. Suddenly Halyn saw his stark reflection in the pane glass of the door to the café. Zach was in line for his coffee. There was no way to avoid him. She had to walk right past him to leave the store. "Maybe I will keep my head down and pretend like I didn't see him." She thought. However, her heart was telling her otherwise. She needed to be the better person, so instead, she planned to say hello to him and then keep on walking. As she approached the door, Zach let out a gentle and inviting smile as he tugged on Halyn's jacket.

"Hi." He said it first.

"Hi," Halyn replied, looking down at her coffee.

There was an awkward silence between them for what felt like an eternity. "Um, I hope you have a good first day back. What class are you off to first?" he asked as he ruffled his hand through his hair nervously.

"Chemistry," Halyn replied confidently, knowing Zach would not be there with her.

"You're a smart cookie. You will ace that class."

"Thanks."

"How about you?"

"I'm not in class until noon today. Just getting my caffeine fix before I head to the gym."

"I see. That's a good way to start the semester." Halyn was getting annoyed with the small talk. The conversation was not going to plan. The plan was in fact to have no conversation or a long, sincere one. But alas after another awkward pause, she gathered up the courage to ask Zach something that she had wanted to ask for a while. "Can we meet up for coffee or something sometime this week to talk?"

"I'm quite busy this week. I have a few priorities going on with school and family and....." He stopped himself, but Halyn knew he was referring to Marissa.

" Ok, maybe next time I guess." She replied, disappointed in her foolishness for asking.

Of course, he wasn't going to meet with her. Why would he? If he wanted to, he would have asked her yesterday, and he always could have sent her a message, knowing they were both back on campus. However, Halyn wasn't able to let go of the fact that she felt as though Zach owed her a conversation at the very least. She had so many unanswered questions that were consuming her mind. On numerous occasions, Rowan told her it was time to move on, but she couldn't. She just wasn't able to understand how anyone, let alone Zach could simply omit another human the way her did, especially to someone he supposedly cared for so deeply. She simply wanted to have the conversation that she felt she deserved. Plus, she wanted to give him the benefit of the doubt that he wasn't just some jerk who would cut his girlfriend off, but instead, maybe there was an understandable underlying reason for his behaviour. At least, this is what she hoped. She couldn't help but repeatedly wonder if she had done something wrong near the end of their relationship and the guilt that came with that possibility lingered. But after hours of replaying every conversation and scenario in her mind, she was not able to recall anything she may have done to be disrespected so heavily.

Halyn walked into class with only one minute to spare, flustered, and emotionally exhausted. She saw Rowan in the front bottom corner of the room, talking to a new student who was sitting beside her. He was fairly attractive, and undeniably Rowan's type, so Halyn decided to make a quiet appearance and sneak into the seat on the other side of her. She was still gabbing away with the guy who's name tag read " Tarek". Rowan turned to Halyn.

" Here's your coffee," Halyn said as she passed the scorching hot beverage to her sister, catching a glance of the new student beside her.

" Thank you. This is Tarek. He's in pre-med as well, just like you. He just transferred here from another school."

Typically, Rowan would have a flirtatious, high-pitched tone to her voice when she was around new testosterone, but she was surprisingly calm and monotone today.

" Hi, I'm Halyn, her sister."

" Sisters in the same class?" Tarek asked, meeting Halyn's gaze.

" We're twins," Halyn said.

" Really? But you don't look much alike at all. I guess if I look closely enough I can see it. Well, I'm happy to meet you Halyn." He didn't take his eyes off of her.

Rowan noticed his immediate attraction to Halyn and she decided to break the ice. " Isn't this a huge class? There must be almost 300 people in here."

"And we all want to be doctors." Tarek and Halyn said simultaneously.

"Not me!" replied Rowan sarcastically.

"What do you want to be?" Tarek asked.

" I haven't decided yet. Rowan replied. I'm just keeping my options open by taking some general classes."

" She wants to be the trophy wife to one of the professors." Halyn chimed in.

" She's only half lying," Rowan stated jokingly.

They opened their books as the professor came in. To their surprise, they were delighted to see Professor Charles walk into the auditorium. He was easy to spot with his royal blue suit and yellow tie.

" Man that guy doesn't miss a beat. It is like he just walked right over here from Milan Fashion Week." Remarked Rowan critically.

There was a moment of silence before Halyn was no longer able to hold her contempt in any longer. " Guess who I just ran into at the café?" she whispered to Rowan.

"Ken or Barbie?"

" Ken. And he looked so good. But in true form, completely blew me off when I asked him to go for coffee this week."

"Of course he's not going to go."

"What do you mean?" Halyn asked angrily

" Because you asked him. You need to wait until

he asks you."

" I know, everyone keeps telling me that, but I'm afraid he's never going to and I'm going to be holding onto this demon forever."

" You just need to move on. Look at Tarek..." Rowan leaned in closer to Halyn. "He's still staring at you. And I don't blame him. You look on point today sista!"

Rowan was right again. For the rest of the class, Tarek was taking quick glances at Halyn, hoping she wouldn't notice him. She was flattered, but not interested in dating anyone, especially since her track record with men wasn't nearly as impressive as her IQ score. She felt like she just couldn't move on until she could talk to Zach. She needed answers. In the back of her mind, she knew perhaps the conversation would never happen and she would potentially never have the answers she longed for.

CHAPTER 11

Halyn ran into Zach often throughout their first semester, each time holding onto deeper resentment and less attraction. She always had butterflies when catching her first glimpse of him, but it quickly fizzled every time he would blow her off. Once in the fall, she ran into him at the gym and the grocery store on the same day and to Halyn's dismay, they did share one class. Luckily it was in the auditorium with many other students, and thankfully, she had Lucy and Becca there to keep her grounded. Each day, Zach would sit at the top of the auditorium directly beside the door and would be the first to leave the class, which never allowed Halyn the opportunity to interact with him. On the last day of the second semester, with her now solid group of girlfriends, Halyn was beginning to move on.

"I'm so happy you've been able to move forward." Said Lucy as Zach walked in and took his seat behind them. He glanced over at Halyn and within a second, diverted his attention to the Professor.

"I am too." Replied Halyn. "A few months ago, all

I could think about was Zach's never-ending rejection. Even though we were within minutes of each other all year, he never offered up the conversation, or the chance to make amends. Now, I'm in a place where I can let go of some anxiety and finally feel like I have built up some of my old confidence again. I'm still not ready to date but at least I'm finding solace in the fact that I can notice a cute guy if one saunters by. Earlier in the year, I would never even take a second glance.

"What about Tarek?" Asked Becca.

"What about him?"

" Would you ever consider dating him?"

"Maybe? I don't know. I would prefer to spend the summer without thinking about the opposite sex. I have plans to travel, go camping and spend almost every sunny day at a beach."

" Sounds like my kind of summer. I can't wait until that bell rings." Said Lucy as she pointed to the analog clock directly above her. " Two more hours until summer break and the end of our second year at Dryden."

Later that week, Halyn and Rowan were packing up their suitcases in the apartment when they heard a violent knock on the door. Both of them looked at each other, motioning for the other to open it. " Maybe they will go away" Halyn thought. But, the person on the other side of the door was persistent and it seemed important. Looking through the peer hole, Rowan was pleasantly surprised to see Tarek standing on the other side. She opened the door.

" Hi. Is Halyn home?" He was breathless and it seemed as though he had run from the other end of campus in record time. Halyn waved from behind Rowan.

" Come in." said Rowan as she gave him a quick hug." He walked right past her.

"Something has come up." He said to Halyn frantically.

" What is it?" Halyn looked at him, concerned. He relaxed at the sight of her. She is so calming and beautiful." He thought to himself. Snapping back to reality, he handed Halyn some wrinkled papers.

"*Summer Research Assistant Needed*". It read.

Halyn looked up at Tarek. Didn't you already have someone lined up for this?"

" Yes, but they backed out at the last minute. I didn't even know who it was at first. It turns out they had hired Marissa Jacobs, and once she found out she actually had to work, she turned the job down."

" How on earth did she ever get the position in the first place?"

" I bet I can guess." Rowan chimed in from the kitchen. " Daddy paid the school. I'm sure of it. Gosh, Marissa is unbelievable and her parents are enablers. There is no way she would have gotten the job based on her grades. She wasn't even in the program for goodness sake!"

"Well, I don't like to be anyone's second choice," Halyn said to Tarek staring his straight in the eye. He broke their gaze. "You'd be perfect for the job. You would be a shoo-in for medical school working under this professor. It will look great on a resume and that's why Marissa wanted the position. The lab didn't want her and they forced her out by making it sound way worse than it is. But they also thought she would back out sooner, so now, the whole lab has their shorts in a knot trying to find the perfect candidate. I told them I had an excellent person in mind, and I came right over."

Tarek was becoming more and more convincing with each sentence. Halyn analyzed his glazed over, hopeful eyes. She had seen eyes like his before. Zach's eyes. Zach was also thoughtful and made her feel special when they were together. Even though she had started to move on, she still had trouble trusting anyone these days. Her head started to spin and she needed to sit down. Tarek sat down beside her, putting his arm around her shoulder. She felt comforted and refrained from pushing him away.

"You need some time to think about it. I can see that. But it won't hurt to just simply go over to the lab and talk to them. This is a huge opportunity for you. You should at least consider it." Tarek's voice was soft and convincing.

Rowan looked at Halyn and nodded in agreement

with Tarek. Halyn rolled her eyes. "You are right." She admitted. "It would be foolish of me to turn this down."

" Great. Why don't I bring you over to the lab? I already know everyone there and can introduce you before you meet with the Professor."

"I guess I'll stay half-packed then?" She looked at Rowan, unsure if she wanted to leave her sister for the summer. They had never spent any significant time apart from one another. This would be new territory for both of them, and her parents were very much looking forward to her return home.

" Don't worry about me," Rowan said reassuringly. You need this, and mom and dad would kill you if you didn't take it. Plus, you'd get to stay in this apartment all by yourself all summer."

" Ok, I'll go. I will need some time to get changed. I don't think a T-shirt and jeans would make the best first impression." Halyn curled her hair and put on a monochromatic gray pant-suit. She jazzed the outfit up with pink floral earrings and black satin shoes with a small heel just high enough to lift her pants off the ground. She quickly glanced in the mirror on her way out of her bedroom, stopping suddenly in her tracks. It was the first time she felt as though her dream of becoming a doctor may come to fruition. She was one step closer and her hard work was paying off. She was appreciative of Tarek's consideration for the job but questioned his motives to some degree.

The lab was in the basement of the science building. Its structure was over one hundred years old, so it was damp and had no windows to the outside, a far cry from a glamorous office space. She knew, however, that if she were to become a doctor, chances were she would be spending a significant amount of time in a similar space and she would have to accept that. Nevertheless, she felt like she was at home. She was surrounded by lab equipment, keen researchers, numbers, and white coats. Tarek didn't look so bad in his white coat either. She was attracted to a man with intellect, and it didn't hurt that he was also handsome. "Being both handsome and smart is so unfair to other guys." She thought.

Throughout the year, she got to know Tarek well. He was in most of her classes and naturally, became a part of her study group. They continued to meet in Halyn's favourite study nook at the library. He would show up with coffee, her favourite snacks and always offered her a walk home. Sometimes, they would stay until the library closed for the night, which was into the early hours of the morning. She didn't realize how much quality time she spent with him, and how similar they were until this moment. He glided along the cement floors of the lab, demure and bold. He was in his element and Halyn found herself attracted to his confidence in the research lab. She smiled as he turned to face her. She retreated her smile and sat in the chair next to her hastily.

She didn't want him to notice her attraction, not just yet, even though a smile could have many meanings.

"What?" He laughed.

"What what? She retorted.

"You're smiling at me. Do I have a Kick Me sign on my back or something?" He did a sarcastic 360 degrees turn looking over his right shoulder.

Halyn chuckled " No, although you are giving me ideas for next year." She followed her chuckle with a wink in his direction.

He smiled back at her, knowing somewhat what she was thinking. "Wait here. I'll go and get Professor Charles."

"Professor Charles?"

" Yes, he's the lead on this study. Are you surprised?"

" I guess a little. I just thought you would have told me that already."

" I thought it might impact your decision to come down. After all, your sister is planning to marry him isn't she?" Tarek winked at Halyn and they shared a brief laugh.

"Oh. Rowan's going to love this." She thought to herself.

Despite slipping up on some words and not being able to produce any references on the spot, Professor Charles offered Halyn the job and she now had a lot to think about. If she took the position, it meant working long hours throughout the summer, unpacking what she had already packed and having a minimal social life. "I guess no camping for me." She thought to herself. Sacrifices were on the horizon with becoming a doctor, and this was just the start. She would spend the summer in virtually no sunlight. But on the other hand, if she turned down the job, she would regret it, and she wouldn't have the chance to work with Tarek, who she was growing fonder of each day. She accepted the offer.

" I'd love to take you out to celebrate," Tarek said nervously as he walked Halyn back to Guildwood.

"Like a date?"

"Do you want it to be a date?"

" I'm not sure I'm ready for that right now. A lot just happened in the last 24 hours."

"Ok, would your friends like to come?"

" I'm sure they would. That's a nice idea. Where to?"

"How about The Orr?"

"Oooooh, fancy pants."

"I'll see if we can even get in."

"Ok, it's a group date."

"Sounds like a plan. And Halyn....?."

" Yes," Halyn swallowed the lump in her throat as they stopped in front of Guildwood..

"Maybe one day it can be just a date." He winked again at her and leaned in to kiss her cheek. He walked away with his hands in his pockets, shoulders shrugged, his full thick hair blowing in the wind. Halyn smiled and ran up the stairs to share the news with her sister.

The Orr was a hotspot for students from Dryden. They had the best seafood Halyn had ever tasted. It was difficult to make a reservation, since it was a restaurant known for its status, and the community in which Dryden sat, was all about status. It was an interesting place for Halyn to people watch. Luckily, Tarek's connection to the lab helped them snag a reservation that night when a cancellation came up. Halyn felt guilty that privilege is what got them the reservation, something she promised herself would not become a regular occurrence. Lucy, Becca, Rowan, Halyn and Tarek ordered a seafood tower with a dozen different flavours of oysters, shrimp, scallops, and sushi. Halyn was in heaven and had let the pressure of the weeks ahead fade for the evening. The girls would be returning home tomorrow, and Halyn wanted to make the night a successful send off and a meaningful way to end the school year. " To Halyn!!" Lucy lifted her glass to toast Halyn's new job.

Just as the others started clinking their glasses, unwanted company arrived. In walked Marissa and Zach, outfits matching, her arm linked with his, scarlet lipstick still on his cheek. Everyone looked at Halyn, including Tarek and he appeared more disappointed than her. Tarek knew that Halyn still wasn't completely over Zach but was hoping that the summer ahead would be a good chance to ask her out on an official date. They would be spending almost all of their time together since most workdays were twelve hours long. He could reassure her that all men weren't self-righteous. On a few occasions, Tarek had witnessed Zach flaunting his new phone, Marissa's cars, his new Rolex, and all along, not realizing that no one else cared except for Marissa. What did Halyn ever see in him? Tarek thought.

" Let's just have a good time." Halyn chimed in, without an ounce of concern on her breath.

Everyone else was surprised. They looked at each other, intrigued by Halyn's nonchalant approach to the issue at hand. " Are you going to be able to eat here with them constantly in your line of vision?" asked Lucy.

"I'm fine." She replied casually, and in fact, she was fine. She ate, drank, and laughed the night away, barely paying any attention to Zach or Marissa. Tarek felt a snippet of hope that maybe Halyn was ready for a date. He recognized that her favourite food was seafood pizza, her eyes were a piercing green, she only had dimples when she laughed and her favourite drink was a chocolate martini. "All details, Zach likely never bothered to notice." He thought to himself.

Tarek was unapologetically in tune with the glances Zach was giving Halyn throughout the night. He was visibly uninterested in Marissa's constant banter. Her arms were flailing in conversation all night and it appeared Zach never got a word in edgewise. At one point, Tarek could hear Marissa ask Zach if "he was even listening to her?" to which he did not reply. Zach's eyes were fixated on Halyn, and then onto Tarek, and for the first time since their breakup, suddenly, Zach was breathing in oxygen and exhaling jealousy. A smirk subconsciously emanated from the corners of Tarek's mouth as he made eye contact with Zach. They stared at each other for a moment, Zach's gaze curious, and Tarek's intrepid.

    Marissa took her last swig of wine and forcefully handed it to the waiter without eye contact, spilling droplets of red wine on his white dress shirt. Zach shook his head. She paid no attention to the waiter, nor Zach's response to her impudent behaviour. He looked over towards the booth again, where Halyn, her sister, and her friends were sitting. He hated that she was having a good time without him, but happy that she had maintained a close friendship with Lucy and Becca. But who was this new guy? And why was he sitting so close to Halyn? He continued to assess Tarek's body language while Marissa kept on yammering about the upcoming weekend and her trust fund.

" So daddy says the private jet will be at the airport at noon tomorrow, so he needs us there for 11:00 AM sharp. I have picked out your outfit for the wedding and packed you some new Gucci shoes." Zach continued to stare over at the booth, not hearing a word Marissa was saying.

" Are you even listening to me?" Marissa yelled. All the patrons surrounding them turned to stare at the couple.

"Well, that certainly got my attention." Zach's face went red with embarrassment. "Why do I need to wear Gucci shoes? What's wrong with the ones I already have?"

" All the single men, married men, and children will be wearing them at the wedding."

" So?"

" So it's expected that you wear them. It is an Italian wedding, and in attendance will be some of the richest and most powerful business moguls in the country. And since you will be with my family, its best to follow the trend. I will have Wilfred come with the Escalade tomorrow and he will pack up the car at 9:00 AM."

Zach looked over at the booth again, Marissa noticing and becoming annoyed at the lack of attention. " Why do you keep looking over at that loser in the booth? Do you know him from somewhere?" She looked over again, except this time, her heart started to pound when she realized Halyn was at the same table. She stood up in a frenzy and threw her napkin on her chair. Without saying a word, she picked up her purse and jacket, Seconds later, Marissa noticed Halyn stand up from the booth and was walking towards the bathroom. Marissa's eyes became fierce. She flipped her hair, smiled, and marched in Halyn's direction, her heels loudly clicking along the concrete floor. All the men in the restaurant stopped to look at her, many of them with dates who were unimpressed. As Marissa turned the corner, Zach thought it would be another opportunity to glance over towards the booth, but Halyn wasn't there. "Shit!" he thought.

Halyn was daydreaming about her new job and the idea of working alongside Tarek all summer when she heard a loud bang on the bathroom stall door. "What on earth?" She opened the door to see Marissa, furious, with sweat beading along her forehead.

"Why are you here? Did you follow us here? You don't even belong in this restaurant anyway." Marissa wasn't holding back.

"I'm having dinner with some friends to celebrate."

"You knew we were coming and you are trying to win him back."

"Sorry Marissa, but that couldn't be farther from the truth. In fact, I'm here with a date, and you should probably get back to yours."

"Who's the guy you are with?"

"None of your business," Halyn responded, keeping her composure.

"He works in the lab where I am working. I recognize him."

"Really? You are going to be working in the

research lab? Because I'm pretty sure you were released from the position that I just started, which is why I'm here, to celebrate. And I didn't pay my way in, I earned it." Halyn glared at Marissa, waiting for her response.

" As far as Zach knows, I'm working there this summer. And you best keep your mouth shut."

" Are you threatening me?" Halyn laughed

" Yes." Replied Marissa. I also plan to tell Zach that you are here with a date. Maybe that way he'll pay attention to me instead of you and your new Geek Prince."

" His name is Tarek, and feel free."

Halyn made her way towards the door. " Oh and Marissa, I'm so sorry to hear there is trouble in paradise." She winked at Marissa and let the door slam shut behind her as she made her way back to the booth. Before she sat down, she put her hand on Tarek's shoulder and gave Zach a concerning glance. He was already staring in her direction. He put his head down in his hands and didn't look back over for the rest of the night.

CHAPTER 12

A week had passed since Marissa and Halyn's restaurant encounter and lately, Zach had started to feel incredibly guilty about that night, and all of last year last year. He was beginning to realize that maybe Marissa's advice had an ulterior motive and that motive, was likely to sabotage his ex. "What does she have against Halyn?" He thought. Maybe it was jealousy since Halyn was tenacious, hard-working, and was achieving her life goals. Or more importantly, maybe it was because she and had a purpose in life that went beyond collecting family money. Zach had concluded that Marissa's only purpose or goal in life, was to inherit a fortune and to flaunt it.

It was Sunday morning, the first official weekend of the summer, but instead of feeling relieved, Zach was feeling conflicted and anxious. He decided to visit Eric since he hadn't seen him all week. Plus, Eric was the only person he could confide in when it came to relationship dilemmas. Eric was the voice of reason in most cases, a "tell it like it is" kind of friend, and he always made a point to make Zach feel better, no matter how down in the dumps he was. Somehow though, today he was nervous to talk to him, afraid of the judgment that might come along with his thoughts. He made his way into the apartment at Guildwood. Eric wasn't there. He hoped to run into Halyn in the hall, but he had no such luck there either. " She must be at work," he thought. " Working with that Derek guy." The more he had thought about Halyn's new love interest, the more he had convinced himself that Tarek was simply a rebound. Zach removed his phone from his back pocket and dialled Eric's number.

"Hello."

Zach was relieved to hear Eric answer the phone. " Hey. Are you going to be home soon?" There was a long, drawn-out pause.

" No, I'm out with the guys."

" How come you didn't invite me?"

" They invited me."

" And you didn't think to call me to see if I wanted to come too? Where are you guys?"

" At the Orr, and honestly, I didn't think you'd be allowed."

Zach's first thought was to react defensively, but he restrained himself knowing that this is what he liked most about Eric, and why he was planning to talk to him in the first place, his brutal honesty.

"Something's been on my mind. I've been in my head all week. I guess I was hoping to run it by you over a beer. I'll head home."

" I'll see you at baseball. We can go grab a beer after." Replied Eric. And he hung up.

Zach hated the short and distant vibe he was picking up from Eric. Based on their conversation, it evidently had to do with Marissa, and Zach never thought that he would be the kind of guy to let a girl get in the way of his friendships.

When Zach arrived back at the lake house, he could hear the smoke detectors going off from the driveway. He frantically ran to the front porch and a puff of smoke blasted him in the face when he opened the front door. " Marissa!! Where are you?" He heard coughing and the sound of the fire extinguisher coming from the kitchen. She had been attempting to cook, which was something Marissa never did for herself. He was both impressed that she had put that much effort into something practical but also disappointed that it didn't work out, since knowing Marissa, she wouldn't want to attempt it again. Marissa couldn't stand failure.

" I was trying to make you dinner." She yelled.

" Here, I've got it." Zach put out the fire in a matter of seconds.

" You're such a hero." She said both literally and sarcastically.

Marissa leaned in and kissed Zach passionately, trying to keep his mind off of the disaster in the kitchen, but to no avail.

"What were you trying to make?"

" Spaghetti Bolognese. And then I went upstairs

for only 5 minutes and I could hear water spilling all over the place. When I came downstairs, the pot and the stove were both burning."

" You have to watch pasta when it is cooking. It can boil over easily."

" Well, obviously I know that now." Marissa changed the subject. " But aren't you so proud of me? I was doing it for you. I thought we could have a little date night in. Of course, now I think its best we go out."

"Maybe we can make it together. Is there any more left? Do you have the ingredients for the sauce out somewhere?" He studied the room as Marissa pointed to the jar of sauce in the pantry. Zach laughed.

" You're cute. It has to go in the fridge once you open it. By the way, I'm going to go for beers with Eric after my game on Friday."

" But that's our pedicure night! Are you sure you can't go the following week?"

" I haven't seen Eric since school ended. I need a night out with my friends."

" What if we did a little of this instead on Friday?" Zach's guard was broken down as Marissa started to run her red-tipped fingernails up and down his chest and began kissing his neck. His heart started beating quickly and he genuinely felt bad for what had just happened in the kitchen. For the first time, she was putting effort into their relationship. Somehow Marissa had found a way to his heart and his head, and though he still felt conflicted about his feelings, she had once again wrapped him around her finger. She was the puppeteer and he was the puppet in a production, he couldn't get out of.

The score was 5-1 in the bottom of the eighth inning and their team was losing. Both Eric and Zach had lost interest in the game, staring at the coach from the other team who appeared to almost be having a heart attack with his constant yelling and cussing. They decided to leave the game early. Zach pre-meditated this plan knowing that he wasn't going to be able to go out after the game.

"Where do you want to go for beers?" Eric asked as he loaded his car with his gear.

" I'm not going to be able to make it. I promised Marissa I wouldn't go out tonight." I can go with you Monday though unless you want to go across the street and grab a quick one now so I'm home when I normally would be."

Eric shook his head, an ominous look on his face.

" Are you upset with me? You've been kind of blowing me off lately." Zach asked

" Seriously bro?" Eric rolled his eyes, shrugging off Zach's burning question.

Arms folded, and leaning against the fence, Zach waited until he was able to get a better response.

"What?" asked Eric now observably annoyed.
Zach waited again.

" Fine. " Eric chimed in reluctantly. " Marissa has cast some kind of spell on you. You always have to go home early and can never come out with the guys. She doesn't come to any of our parties or study groups because we just aren't good enough for her. It's annoying and you are a different person now.

" What happened to me dating Marissa Jacobs and now I don't have to worry about anything?" asked Zach defensively.

" I never said you don't have to worry about anything. I said you don't have to worry about other girls. But maybe you do need to worry about this one. You were the one who called me and wanted to talk remember? And now, I'm here to talk and you can't because you have to go home and get your toes polished with your girlfriend. "

"Well, when you put it that way, it does sound kind of bad." They both laughed.

"That's what I wanted to talk about with you anyway. I'm not sure how I feel about Marissa. I think I may still have feelings for Halyn."

" Ooooh, a love triangle! Have you told Halyn?"

" Dude, of course not. Besides she's dating that Marek guy, or whatever his name is."

" Tarek." Eric corrected Zach. " And he's a really smart guy. He was a lab assistant for one of my classes."

"You aren't helping me right now Eric."

" Ok, well, who do you see a future with?" asked Eric as he threw his gear in the car.

It was a burning question, one that caught Zach completely off guard, and he was surprised that he had never thought of it himself. A month ago he would have confidently said Marissa, since she was providing him with a lavish lifestyle of vacations, cars, gourmet food, and sex. Now, he wasn't so sure. Marissa was beautiful and exciting. But Halyn was comfortable and easy. With Marissa, he felt like he always had to look and act his best, but the money and sex were great. With Halyn, he could completely be himself. He could be vomiting and wearing last night's jogging pants and she still adored him. She took care of him, was loving and selfless. Most of all, her vulnerability and intellect were his favourite of her many impressive qualities.

Zach moved over towards Eric and leaned his head back against the fence, looking up at the cloud-filled sky. It was about to rain. His breathing became shallow and quick, sweat dripping down his forehead. He looked at Eric, and Eric met his gaze.

"It's Halyn isn't it?" Eric asked

"I think so." And just then, the cloud above them burst open, sending a stream of rain downward, drenching Zach as he sat against the fence until he left to be back at the lake house on time.

CHAPTER 13

Halyn took one last look at the specimen under the microscope, before setting down her pen and notepad for the night, her eyes, crossing after several hours of staring and focusing through a tiny lens. She was exhausted, and lonely. No one else was in the lab all day and she was without a ray of sunlight, except for the fifteen-minute walk she took on her solo lunch break. She outstretched her arms and then packed her belongings as quickly as she could, so she could get outside before the sun fully set. Just as she was about to turn off the lights of the lab, she heard a whistle on the other side of the door. Perplexed, she inched her head outside into the hallway, pleasantly surprised to see Tarek around the corner. He was dressed casually in jeans and a V-neck T-shirt, handsome in his simplicity.

"Well hello." She said, trying not to appear too excited.

" Well hello yourself. I was coming to free you from this dismal abyss. How long have you been in this room?"

" Ten hours." Halyn opened the door for Tarek

and he slowly made his way in towards her. Halyn's heart skipped a beat, as she sighed loudly.

" Did I do something wrong?" He asked perplexed.

" No quite the opposite. You are a pleasant sight to see after staring at microbes for ten hours. " She leaned in to embrace Tarek. They closed their eyes in unison, absorbing the chemistry between them.

" People will start to think you are a vampire if you never get out of here. Let's go out somewhere."

"What do you suggest?"

" Have you eaten yet?"

" Not since noon. I could use something to eat."

" Let's hit up a patio since you haven't been outside at all this week. Let's celebrate a little TGIF! We both could use it."

" Like a real date?" Halyn asked

Excitement emanated from Tarek's face. " You just made my day, maybe even my year."

" It's a date then." Halyn smiled at him through pursed lips as she grabbed her bag and then his hand.

A thick blanket of sweltering heat hit Halyn like a ton of bricks as she walked outside. The sun was just setting and she breathed a sigh of relief at the thought of having a day off the next day. Seeing that all of her summer plans were now on hold, she wanted to pack her free days with beach trips, camping, and patios. But, most of all, she wanted to spend as much time as she could with Tarek, to test the waters on where their relationship stood, and where it could potentially go. She was ready but also hesitant to jump in full force for many reasons. Her last two relationships were a flop, to say the least, and although she had strong feelings for Tarek, she still wasn't able to fully let go of Zach. No matter how hard she tried, the thoughts of his betrayal and lack of apology flooded her mind. She couldn't understand it. And with a lack of explanation or reason behind it, it made the situation far more confusing. If he could have on one occasion, simply sat down and talked to her, maybe she could have some closure and it would clear her mind. But up until this point, he had denied all the requests she had sent him.

Tarek escorted Halyn, hand in hand to one of her favourite patios. It was a rooftop patio on campus, above the Central Hub. The Central hub was the centerpiece of Dryden's school grounds. It housed the main food court, pubs, bars, and the gym was even located in its basement. It was incredibly quiet since most students were away for the summer, but still, the atmosphere was vibrant and the fresh air was welcoming to Halyn. They made their way to a table that was situated close to the edge of the patio, where they could see the entire campus and the sun setting along the horizon. Tarek pulled Halyn's chair back and ordered them each a drink.

"You aren't wasting any time," Halyn remarked

" I just want to start enjoying the weekend, and I'd prefer to spend more time talking to you, rather than the server."

Halyn smiled as Tarek sat down into his seat. She was admiring his casual character and confidence. " What time do you have to work Sunday?" She asked.

" Let's not talk about work. We have all summer to do that. How about we talk about what you'd like to do tomorrow, and about us," he suggested, peering meekly over his glass of gin and tonic.

Halyn admired that even though he barely had any time off throughout the summer, he was more concerned about what she wanted to do. There were no selfish bones in his body. " Well, I'd love to go to the beach. But let's do something you would like to do as well."

" I'm just happy being with you, wherever we are. I could be in a mud trench or a dump and I'd still feel like the luckiest guy on earth."

" Or stuck in a cold basement in a building with no windows?" She asked sarcastically.

He laughed. "Yes or that too. I get excited when I wake up in the morning knowing I get to work beside you. It's been making me think a lot lately."

"About what?"

"Us."

" What about us specifically?" Halyn became nervous, she took a deep breath to calm herself.

" Well, are we dating? Are we exclusive? Or are we in the friend zone?"

Halyn wasn't prepared for such a loaded question, nor did she want to answer him immediately. He was completely invested in them as a couple. But the more she thought about it, she more than understood the turmoil of unanswered questions and disappointment, so she thought she owed it to Tarek, to be honest with him. If anything positive came of her breakup with Zach, it was the lessons she had learned of what not to do to someone you care about.

" I was hoping to explore our relationship over the summer. You are aware of what I went through last year, and I just need to take things slow. I like you a lot and I get excited to see you every day too. I love our time together, but I just want to make sure I'm certain of my feelings for you before I commit to anything."

Disappointment set in as Tarek stared blankly at Halyn. " You are unsure of your feelings? Why does it have to be complicated? Do you like spending time with me?"

"Yes. I just said I did."

" Do you think of me when you wake up and before you fall asleep at night?"

"Yes, often."

" Do you miss me when I'm not with you?"

"Yes."

" Then what more do you need to know?"

" I need to know that my heart won't be broken again. I'm quite guarded now, more than ever. And I need to be able to get out of my head before I can commit to you or any other serious relationship. It wouldn't be fair to either of us. Halyn picked up Tarek's hand, clasping it tightly into hers.

" I'm not saying that I don't want to date you or be your girlfriend. I just need time. It's only been a few weeks that we have been spending time together. I jumped into my last relationship and it backfired. I want to be fair to both of us. I promise I won't string you along and I know that if it starts to get serious, then its time for that next step, but for now, let's casually date and get to know each other better. Is that fair?

At first, Tarek seemed hesitant, but then he decided to lighten the mood and go with it." Ok. I'll start."

"Start what?"

" To get to know you. What's your favourite movie?"

Halyn held Tarek's other hand, gazing into his eyes, instantly letting some of her guards down." Anything Disney." She replied confidently, knowing the judgment that might follow.

" Cute. I love The Lion King."

"Classic." They both laughed.

" What about you? She asked?"

" Back to the Future. "

Halyn chuckled. " Another classic" she replied. " What's your favourite food?"

" Chicken wings.....with beer."

" And your favourite color? Sport?"

"Black and baseball."

" Really? Black? It's not even a color."

" I look good in black." He lifted his eyebrows repeatedly, breaking down Halyn's guard even more.

" Ok, do you have any dirty little secrets?"

" Oh, we are going there are we?" Tarek took a swig of his drink, his eyes widening.

Suddenly Halyn realized, she was asking all the questions. " Why aren't you asking me anything?" She gave him a nudge to the shoulder.

" Because I already know the answer to all of the questions you asked. Your preferred color is purple, your food of choice is seafood pizza, your favourite sport is soccer and your dirty little secret is that your parents paid for your fancy apartment." Halyn slapped him in the shoulder this time, rather than a nudge. " I deserved that." He said.

Halyn was strikingly impressed by Tarek's attention to detail. He had studied her and completely out of genuine interest. With every passing minute, she couldn't help but fall for him more. She took a sip of her drink and stared off the patio and onto the horizon, slightly disappointed that it was almost dark. She shivered as a brisk wind blew her tousled hair into her eyes. Tarek reached over and moved her hair, just the way Zach did. She froze for a moment, remembering his touch. She forced it out of consciousness and re-focused on Tarek, the man who had noted all of her favourites, who came to rescue her from work, and who was sincerely committed to her.

The night flew by quickly. Halyn finished her drink, then yawned. Looking down at her watch, it made sense. Normally, she was going to sleep now. " Thank you for bringing me here," she said honestly. " It was exactly what I needed. I think I should head home now."

" Already? We don't have to work tomorrow. You will be able to count on one hand the number of days we have off this summer."

" Exactly, you don't want me tired and grumpy for tomorrow. I'm looking forward to it."

"Me too." Tarek stared at Halyn, with slight disappointment in his eyes. " Ok let's go." He stood up and removed his jacket, placing it over Halyn's shoulders as she shivered in the breeze. He took a moment to study her, wishing he could get inside her head. Lately, he found her hard to read, mostly because she was usually uncomplicated and simple. She didn't have room for drama in her life and focused on her career and future and he admired her for it.

As they stepped onto the cobblestone walkway outside of the Central Hub, Halyn was feeling guilty for cutting their night short, and she could feel Tarek's dismay emanating through the thick, damp air. She decided that she would make their day off a special one. Plus, she still hadn't done anything to thank him for the job yet, and she knew it would be the perfect opportunity to further explore their relationship. He was also correct in his assessment of their upcoming summer, free time was going to be limited and she was perfectly fine spending it with Tarek.

" I promise tomorrow will be fun." She kissed him on the cheek. He pulled her in, and kissed her on the lips, holding her face in the palms of his hands. She melted underneath his touch. He was a good kisser. As he released her gently from his hands, he skimmed his way down the soft skin of her arm until he reached the base of her hand, clasping it firmly. " I'll walk you home."

" I'd like that." Halyn's body has frozen in place, a surge of excitement rose through her body as Tarek kissed her. It was like nothing else she had ever felt before. It felt comfortable and right. She didn't want it to end.

They walked in silence for a moment, enjoying the gardens and scenery along the way. " You make me feel really good. I haven't been this into someone in a long time," he said to her, admiring her confident gait. She didn't respond but simply smiled with appreciation. They stopped at the top of the steps at Guildwood, only one spotlight shining onto Tarek's face. Halyn kissed him again, except this time, she reciprocated his passionate kiss, and she meant it and it felt just as good as the last.

"I will pick you up in the morning?" He asked.

"I'll be waiting with bells on."

"How about a bikini? Bells might not be enough for the beach."

They both laughed as Tarek let go of Halyn's hand and watched her walk through the door until she was out of sight. Halyn rummaged through her purse, frantically looking for her keys. She knelt onto the floor and removed all of her items onto the floor, a slight feeling of panic running through her chest. Her keys were missing. She took a second look, displacing the objects from her purse onto the floor. Nothing.

"Great!" She shouted out loud. She was about to call Tarek when she heard a voice from the top of the stairs.

"Looking for these?" It was Eric and he was dangling her keys over the ledge atop of the staircase, a smug maniacal grin on his face like he was holding a precious heirloom. Halyn didn't give in to his facetiousness. She walked us the stairs towards him, breathing a sigh of relief.

"Yes. Thank you, Eric." She reached for the keys. He pulled them back in hesitation.

"What are you doing?" She asked as her frustration rose again.

"What's going on with Tarek? You two looked pretty cozy out there.

"I don't see how that's any of your business." She reached for the keys again.

"Got something to hide?" He pulled them back.

"What do you mean?"

"I mean if you don't have anything to hide, then you would just tell me right?"

"We're just hanging out." Halyn kept her eyes on her keys, tracking them as Eric flailed them around in the air.

"That looked like more than just hanging out to me. He pointed towards the door. Clearly, Eric had seen their romantic exchange.

"Yes. We are just dating. I'm interested in him, but I'm hesitant."

"Because of Zach?" He asked. Halyn wasn't prepared for Eric to be so blunt.

"Yes."

"Well, if it makes you feel any better, I'm on your side with this one. But you need to stop texting and messaging him all the time."

"I'm sorry?"

"He told me you have been sending him messages for a while now."

"You mean when we broke up? Or hold on wait….you mean when I reached out to him several times so he could have the decency to break up with me in person? Or maybe give me some explanation as to why he just blew me off, like I didn't even exist anymore. Every single one of my messages was for that purpose, to try and start the conversation, hoping that maybe, he would at least try and make me feel somewhat better about the situation. You both need to get over your egos. My texts and messages are for no other purpose than to get the explanation I deserve and have deserved for a long time."

"Do you ever see yourself with him again?"

"What???" She shook her head in disbelief. "Do you hear at all what I'm saying?"

"Yes I hear your words, but I can also hear your emotions. Your words aren't matching up with your emotions. I can tell you still like him."

Halyn stared at him, with anger in her eyes. Her anger softened as she slowly lowered herself to the ground and sat on the top step of the grand staircase. Eric sat beside her and hugged her.

"I'm sorry. It's just that I kind of wish you two were still together too. Marissa is a nightmare. I barely see the guy anymore."

"I'm sorry to hear that." Halyn replied " But I don't feel bad for him. He knew exactly the kind of person she was going into it. And quite frankly she's the last person I want to talk about.

"You didn't answer my question. Could you ever see yourself with him again?"

" I don't know. That's not an easy question for me to answer. Right now, I would have to say no because I was so betrayed by him. I don't know if I could see myself with someone who feels okay doing that to me. And I certainly don't want to risk it happening again. I have a guard like Fort Knox up right now, and it's affecting all of my other relationships." She paused for a moment, her mind swirling. Are you asking for yourself or him?"

Eric went silent, unsure how much information to give her, but she picked up on his hesitation.

"Eric, do you know something I don't?"

This time, he took a long pause, hoping to deflect the conversation, but he was unsuccessful. He sighed heavily looking over at Halyn who had hope in her eyes and she probably didn't even know it.

"Look, all I can say is that we men, boys, whatever you want to call us, make mistakes. We don't think before we make important decisions all the time, and sometimes, like most humans, we don't realize what we have until something is gone. Are you catching my drift?"

Halyn dropped her head into her hands. She could feel her heart ripping in two different directions. It was obvious that Eric had some inside information on Zach's state of mind. He was regretfully confused. "Why hasn't he talked to me about it?" she asked. Why does he continue to ignore me?

"I don't know. Probably because you are both interested in other people and it would be inappropriate to interfere. Regardless of how you feel about the situation, he was really into you."

"I'm not sure I agree. I could never treat someone I care about like that. Eric, one day he was literally talking about our future, and then the next complete silence, for weeks, like I didn't even exist. Do you know how hurtful that is? So back to your question, the answer is no. I couldn't see myself with him, even though my heart is telling me he could potentially be my soul mate. And the simple reason is that I just don't think I could ever trust him again, and that's heavy."

Eric had no words. Inside, he agreed with her, but due to "bro code" he couldn't admit it. " I'm glad we talked." He said.

" Me too." Replied Halyn. " Can I have my keys back now? I desperately need sleep."

Eric handed her the keys and he helped her stand up off the top step of the staircase.

"Good night Eric," Halyn said, exasperated.

"Night."

Halyn closed the door behind her as she walked into the apartment. All the lights were off and she would only see the flickers of campfires from across the lake. She leaned back against the door and began to sob. Her heart was racing and she certainly wasn't going to get any sleep anytime soon. Her phone rang. She looked down into the palm of her hand to see that it was Tarek calling. She didn't answer it. Instead, she waited for it to go to voicemail and then she dialled Rowan's number but she didn't answer.

Even though she only had four solid hours of sleep, Halyn decided that she owed it to Tarek to follow through with their date. She didn't know what he had planned and although the events of the previous night were consuming her mind, she was looking forward to a day out. It was a beautiful sunny and humid summer day. Halyn watched several boats coast across the crystal blue lake outside of her window while she sipped her green tea. She sat in her floral sundress waiting for Tarek to pick her up and had put on a little extra makeup attempting to hide the evidence from her lack of sleep. He would certainly want to know why she was so tired since she went home early. Her gaze across the lake was interrupted by a knock at her door. As she made her way across the room, she noticed a pink piece of paper slip under her door and land at her feet. She picked up the paper, perplexed as to what it could be. In Tarek's neat handwriting it read:

> ***"Meet me downstairs in 20 minutes.***
> ***Bring sunscreen."***

A large, uneven heart was drawn around the note in red marker. Tarek was exactly what her heart needed and she couldn't help but smile at his note. He was concerned about her getting a sunburn. Luckily she had already packed her sunscreen in her beach bag, assuming they would be heading to the beach or a park at some point in the day. She put on a simple pair of flip-flops and made her way downstairs and outside onto the sidewalk. Tarek wasn't there, but she had three minutes to spare. Her phone buzzed as a message came through. Her heart began pounding when she read Zach's name on her screen. Halyn had to look down at her phone a few times to confirm that she wasn't seeing things. At that moment, Tarek came racing around the corner, two lattes in hand. Halyn put her phone into her beach bag without reading the message and displaced it to the back of her mind.

" Hi! " She greeted Tarek excitedly, jumping into his arms, almost spilling both of their drinks.

" Well hello to you too." Tarek was surprised by Halyn's excitement.   " Why the overzealous greeting?"

" What do you mean? Can't I be excited to see you?"

" Well, you certainly have a lot of energy. Must be all that sleep you got last night.

Halyn hesitated before changing the subject. " Thanks for the note this morning. It was cute and a pleasant surprise. It made me even more excited for our date today."

" That's what I was hoping for. Ready to go?"

"Yes. Where are we going?"

"I thought we could have a little breakfast."

" Great. I'm starving. Where did you have in mind."

" Come with me." He clasped Halyn's hand and

led them around the building towards a white convertible car. He stopped beside the front passenger seat, retrieving the keys from his pocket, pressing the button at the top of the key. The doors of the convertible clicked open.

"No! Is this your car?" She asked in amazement.

"Not exactly. I rented it for the weekend. But maybe we could have one like this someday." He winked at her and proceeded to open the door, motioning her in.

"Oh my, this is fantastic." Halyn crouched down onto the bright red leather seats that still had a new car smell. "

"Have you ever ridden around in such a fine piece of work before?" Tarek asked as he climbed into the driver's seat. He was grinning from ear to ear, and Halyn quickly learned he had a passion for cars. He was like a kid at Christmas.

"Not that I can recall, but I'm ok to start now." Suddenly, she was interested in cars too.

"Perfect. But before we get going, we are missing something important." Tarek reached down below the steering wheel holding down a silver switch. The humming of the roof startled Halyn as it began to lift off of the car, exposing the blue sky above them. Tarek reached over placing his arm around Halyn's shoulders. Normally, she would be hesitant with such a commanding gesture, but at this moment, she was smitten with Tarek's effort, and for the first time in months, she felt a strong surge of butterflies in the pit of her stomach. Good butterflies. As they drove off campus, Halyn couldn't help but smile from ear to ear. She pulled Tarek in closer to her, until his hand was around her arm. She put her hand in his as they drove off-campus.

In the distance, Zach watched as Halyn drove off with another man, his heart sinking. He stood frozen at the edge of the sidewalk, wishing he hadn't witnessed what he just saw.

CHAPTER 14

Zach looked down at his phone and opened the message he had previously sent to Halyn. Disappointed, he realized that it remained unread. Although he was supposed to be on his way home from the gym, he now certainly wasn't in the mood to face Marissa. She had been particularly unpleasant ever since she learned that Halyn was chosen in place of her for the lab assistant position. She had yet to reveal this deceit to Zach, but he found out through his friends. Whenever she alleged to be off to work in the morning, Zach knew she was going to the spa or the beach for the day. She would leave the house with her beach bag on her shoulder, and a bathing suit under her dress.

Marissa had also recently been vocal about her judgemental opinions of Halyn and her sister, all unwarranted and it was really starting to get to Zach. Her true colors were now exposed, and even worse, recently she was contemplating dropping out of school altogether and not finishing her last year, claiming her father would give her an executive position as one of his companies someday anyway. The nepotism was nauseating and certainly not the vibe he needed to go home to at this moment. He turned around in the opposite direction he was traveling and made his way into Guildwood instead.

    Eric had informed Zach of his talk with Halyn yesterday, hence why he felt the urgency to send her a message. He was anxious to know how she would perceive it. Based on what Eric had told him, he couldn't get a clear idea of what she may be thinking. All he knew was that he needed to approach the subject delicately and that she left the conversation with Eric, holding the weight of unanswered questions. He also didn't want to lead her on or give her any idea that he was seriously regretting his actions from months ago. He needed to play it cool and slowly win her back.

    Eric answered the door in only a pink towel. Zach hesitated, giving Eric a concerned look before laughing uncontrollably at his friend. "Pink? Been to any baby showers lately?" Zach asked sarcastically as he tossed his gym bag on the floor, helping himself to a sport drink in the fridge.

"Dude, I'm on a student budget. It's my mom's."

"And there were no other color options?"

"I'm comfortable enough in my own skin to wear pink. And no, I didn't have a lot of choices."

"I've seen your mom's house so I believe you. Now can you put some clothes on?"

"Why?"

"Because A, I can't take you seriously, right now,

and B, I need you to come to the beach with me this afternoon."

Eric went to his room to change, as they carried on their conversation between the exposed brick walls. "You seem like you are on a mission. Does this have anything to do with my conversation with Halyn? Did you message her?"

"Yes to both."

Eric appeared around the corner wearing his swim trunks and a surf shirt, his long curly hair tied up in a bun.

" What's happening to you? First a pink towel and now a man bun?"

"Will you stop judging me?"

Zach could see that Eric was becoming offended by his banter, so he decided to change the subject back to the issue at hand. "I saw her leave with Tarek this morning in a convertible. My heart was in my throat. I was speechless and nauseous. I'm not sure I can watch her develop feelings for this guy."

" I think you're a bit too late bro. She seems pretty into this guy. And I can tell he's falling head over heels for her. The guy was drooling all over her last night."

" Eric, Normally I appreciate your blatant honesty, but you aren't helping right now."

"Sorry."

" Anyway, I saw her with a beach bag and she was wearing her bathing suit. She loves the beach, so

I'm sure they are headed there."

"Oh so now we are stalking her are we?"

"No, not stalking. I just need to assess how serious this relationship is."

"That's stalking dude, but I'll do it. I can handle taking the day to look at girls in bikinis. You owe me coffee for a week."

"Deal."

The waves were crashing along the jagged stone wall of the pier as Halyn and Tarek parked the convertible along the shoreline, where the pier met the sandy beach. Halyn breathed in and the cool, dry air filled her lungs and calmness consumed her body. Her mind had been racing back and forth between Zach's impending message and Tarek's charm. She kept her phone in her bag for the entire ride, knowing that she wanted to focus on Tarek. She admired him for a moment, unable to control herself from becoming immersed in his perfect presence. He was in a dry fit muscle tank top, exposing his exquisitely chiselled biceps. Ray Ban sunglasses covered his crystal blue eyes, and his hair was messy, which suited him. She was becoming increasingly attracted to him, and not because of their shared love of academics, and his undeniable effort and charm, but she was attracted to who he was as a person. She liked that he didn't feel the need to be anyone else. He was authentic and genuine, and that was all too hard to find in the 21st century.

Climbing out of the car, Tarek motioned for Halyn to remain seated. She grinned. She liked it when he took charge. He opened her door and reached out his hand. She met his grasp and kept holding his hand as he picked up her beach bag and walked along the shoreline. The water was warmer than Halyn had expected. She grazed her feet through the light brown sand, picking up seashells along the way, placing them strategically in the pocket of her sundress for safe keeping.

" Do you always do that when you go to the beach?"

" No, just today. I want to save them, for us. I'm going to make a little something with them and put them in my room."

Tarek grasped Halyn's hand a little tighter. He turned her briskly towards him, grabbing onto her chin with his other hand, and kissed her boldly. She melted in his hands. He was holding her chin, a gesture that she had only dreamed of until now, and it was everything she had imagined. She also was not used to the public display of affection, but for the first time, she wasn't concerned about the onlookers' judgments. She instead chose to savour the moment and let him kiss her without hesitation. She felt fireworks and didn't want to let him go. So she didn't, she pulled him in tighter, reaching around his waist until what felt like his entire body was against hers.

" I think we need to find a private spot on this beach," he whispered, resting his forehead on hers. His palms were sweaty and his heart was racing. They walked to the furthermost point of the beach, where a willow tree hung over a small area of sand that jutted out into the lake. Behind it, a small dune provided them with an intimate cove of privacy, just enough space to lay out a blanket. Tarek had come prepared, and much to Halyn's amusement, he pulled out a larger than life-sized beach blanket, with enough space to fit an entire family, as well as a container of watermelon that had leaked throughout the interior of his backpack. Halyn giggled, and Tarek's cheeks flushed instantly.

"It's ok. I know what to get you for Christmas now." She eyed the old cracked plastic container that held their now dehydrated watermelon."

He playfully motioned her towards the ground and kissed her forehead. They were both silent for a while, Tarek staring into Halyn's eyes, her pupils dilating. Suddenly, he knew his feelings for her were being reciprocated as they continued to make out under the willow tree in their private haven on the beach.

" Can I ask you something?" Tarek's voice wavered as they came up for air. Halyn opened her eyes, certain he was about to ask an intimate question. "Sure."

He hesitated, choosing his words wisely before asking. " Is it only because of your last relationships that you are so reserved and afraid to fully commit to me? Or is there something else I should know?"

Halyn absorbed the question calmly, calculating her response and rehearsing it in her mind before answering. " Mostly yes, but I've also witnessed my parent's struggles over the years, and it's in my character. I'm just a reserved person I guess." She could see that her answer did not suffice based on his expression. He was perplexed or maybe even utterly confused. " What are your parents like?" She asked, attempting to switch the focus onto him and to Halyn's surprise, a smile lit up his face.

" They are pretty much as good as parents can get I think. I'm lucky. They are the epitome of love and commitment. I can only hope to have half the relationship that they do, which seems perfect on the outside to most people, including me, but it can also be daunting because it sets the bar high, you know?"

"Yes, I can see that," Halyn answered honestly.

" My dream is to end up with someone that they approve of, where they can see that same kind of love in my eyes. I know if they approve of whoever I decide to end up with, I'm in good hands. I trust their opinion. After all, they are the gold standard for old married people."

Halyn laughed. " Are they really old?"

" No." Tarek chuckled. " Old compared to us I guess."

" It's nice to hear that you have such a tremendous amount of respect for them. That's hard to find nowadays."

" I know, and I like you a lot Halyn and I hope I can find that someday with you. I wish I could freeze this moment forever."

Halyn paused, as she took a bite of the last piece of watermelon. She had never had anyone speak to her so honestly and with so much conviction in their voice. His eyes were sincere and respectful. She felt as though her guarded walls were crumbling within her body. "I see some great potential in us." Realizing the magnitude of her sentence, she took a deep breath and realized that she was fully committing herself to date Tarek at that moment.

Zach continued to patrol the soft, white sand beach frantically searching for Halyn. He was determined to find out what kind of chance he still had with her if he had one at all. Another message from Marissa appeared on his phone, along with five missed phone calls. Knowing that the harassment wasn't going to end, he decided to message her back. As he was typing his message, the phone rang again. He groaned apathetically before reluctantly answering it.

"Hi, Marissa."

" Why aren't you answering my calls? And why aren't you home yet? We are being picked up in less than an hour to head to the Hamptons."

" I don't think I'm going to make it. I'm helping

Eric out. He's in a bind."

" With what? What could be more important than going to the Hampton's?"

"Lots of things Marissa."

"I expect you home in twenty minutes! Eric can see you next weekend!"

She was shouting so loudly, he had to pull his phone away from his ear. He tried to calm her. " I'm not coming Marissa. Go spend some time with your family. It will be good for you."

Unfortunately, Zach knew that being with her family would only exacerbate her entitled behaviour, since this weekend, they were discussing her trust fund and potential positions for Marissa with one of the family businesses. As tempting as a lifestyle for the rich and famous was, he was beginning to realize that things weren't always what they seemed. Being a part of the Jacobs family was more like a prison, and Zach knew he could never be his true self or lead his own life if he stayed with Marissa. Becoming a member of her family meant that she owned him and that her family's money controlled his every move. She was possessive enough already, and he knew he had to end their relationship before it got out of hand.

" We need to talk when you get back." He said without any further delay.

Marissa hung up the phone abruptly. Zach sighed heavily and motioned his fingers through his hair. With the deep sigh came a massive feeling of relief, a huge weight lifting off of his shoulders. He felt free, a feeling he hadn't experienced in months. He didn't realize how tight of a leash Marissa had on him until now. However, at the moment, his most important mission was to find Halyn, the one who he was meant to be with. He missed everything about her. He missed her simple, caring nature, the way she took care of him when he was sick, and how angelic she looked sitting by the fireplace in the library.

He reached into his back pocket, pulling out the guitar pick Halyn had given him almost two years prior. He frowned knowing Halyn was not aware that he was still carrying it with him daily. Not only because it was all he had left of her, but also because he knew its value, and what it meant to her. It was no Rolex or extravagant car, but it was more precious than both of those combined. It was this gift, the guitar pick that scared him away in the first place, but it was also what was drawing him back to her now. He never appreciated what they had. His uncertainty and panic took over all those months ago, and now more than ever, he wished that he had the guts to fight away his fear of commitment when he had the chance. " Idiot." He thought to himself, as he threw a smooth, flat stone into the water. He turned towards a large willow tree in the distance. It was situated on a quiet alcove at the far end of the beach, and it didn't look like anyone was in its vicinity. He needed some space to think about what he would say to Halyn if he were to see her today. Eric was making his way towards Zach, sunscreen, and towel in hand. Zach motioned towards the willow tree. Let's go over there." He said. They walked slowly along the shoreline. The water was warmer than Zach thought it would be. It was cooler on the side of the lake where Marissa lived, in the lake house, which Zach couldn't wait to move out of. But where would he go? Moving in with Eric certainly was not an option. Living down the hallway from Halyn would be too onerous, and would imply desperation. He decided to worry about that later.

    A taintless sand dune sat beneath a breathtakingly large willow tree. Zach decided to climb the dune rather than walk around it. He could see a large, rustic freight ship on the horizon. As the sand appeared in his line of vision below the dune, he caught a glimpse of a pair of feet, sprawled along a tousled blanket. Pausing under the trees lining the beach, he felt them move. The highest boughs of the willow roared in the wind, as a warning and an invitation. Immediately, his heart started to pound. His worst fear came true when he raised his head overlooking the other side of the dune. Under the large willow tree were Tarek and Halyn, in each other's arms, kissing and she was relishing it……him……… the man who had stolen her. Their eyes were both closed, so luckily they didn't see him. Zach fell to the ground on the other side of the sandy hill, his head extending back until it hit the hard sand. Shutting his eyes firmly, he clenched his fists as Eric put his hand on his friend's shoulder, hoisting him off the ground. They both walked away without looking back. Zach deleted his message he had sent Halyn earlier that day as the wind's speed and fervour picked up.

CHAPTER 15
2 years later

The first word on the intimidating transcript spoke volumes. For weeks, Halyn's heart had sat in her throat anticipating this moment. Everything she had worked for had finally paid off.

CONGRATULATIONS! ....

Unable to collect her thoughts, she stopped reading and put the coarse paper on the table face up. She read the first line again. Halyn Curtis had been accepted into medical school. It was her dream come true. Her mother reached over to her daughter, a proud ego enveloping Halyn's chest, hugging her tightly, with tears in her eyes. " We must celebrate!" She exclaimed as she released the embrace and raced for the kitchen to open a bottle of champagne.

" Great job sis. I knew you could do it." Rowan hugged Halyn tightly. " But what will I do without you next year? We've never spent a school year apart."

"I guess you will just have to visit us."

" Us?" Her mother questioned her from the inside of the refrigerator door.

Halyn looked over her shoulder, nervously directing Tarek to move forward and stand beside her. "Yes. Us. Tarek and I have decided to move in together."

"Yay!" cried Becca

"I knew it." Said Lucy. I knew he'd go along with you if you got in.

" Well, there is more news." Replied Tarek. I just took a position at the university as an associate professor in the science program. I'll be working in the building right next door to the medical school. I can't wait. And there is so much more to look forward to."

"There is?" Halyn asked. What else? What am I missing?"

Tarek pivoted towards Halyn, grasping both of her hands in his and he looked deeply into her eyes. He was trembling. " Halyn Curtis, you have been the best addition to my life over the last three years. In fact, you are my whole life and I would like to spend the rest of it with you.

Whether it's in a lab, at the beach, in your parent's home, or the hospital lunchroom while you are working long hours, I know in the deepest parts of my soul, that I couldn't bear a day without you. I want to grow old with you and you make me a better person each and every minute that I am lucky enough to spend with you." Tarek reached into his pocket and pulled out a gray velvet box. He stumbled down onto one knee, almost falling to the floor, his legs felt like jelly. As he opened the box, revealing a solitary emerald cut ring, he looked into her eyes and asked" Will you marry me Halyn?"

Everyone in the room gasped simultaneously. Lucy and Becca had to sit down due to shock and Rowan was bursting at the seams. Tears filled Halyn's eyes, her cheeks were flushed and her mind was running a mile a minute. She stared at Tarek for a few seconds, which felt like an eternity to him.

"Yes. I'd love to marry you." Halyn replied as she started to giggle uncontrollably. Reactively, Tarek got to his feet and lifted Halyn off the ground in his embrace. He spun her around until they both collapsed onto the couch in a long romantic kiss, their legs intertwined as he placed the ring on Halyn's left hand.

" Save it for the Honeymoon," interrupted her father. Halyn and Tarek respected his wishes and pulled apart from each other, still interlocking arms while Halyn admired her new ring.

"You don't seem the least bit surprised by this dad. Did you know?" Halyn asked, knowing the answer already simply by reading his expressionless face.

"I did. He asked for my blessing a couple of weeks ago. But the moment was better than I had anticipated."

Halyn was charmed by Tarek's gentlemanlike qualities. Not many men would ask their girlfriend's dad for their hand in marriage nowadays. But she had scored herself a true man, a keeper, who she had just devoted herself to for the rest of her life, and on top of that, she had been accepted into medical school on the same day.

Halyn's mother appeared from the kitchen with a tray of half-filled champagne flutes garnished with strawberries along the rims. Small napkins reading "Congrats" accompanied the drinks. She raised her glass "Let's toast to the happy couple. To a long life together, success and the pitter-patter of feet that I can call my grandchildren."

"Really mom?" Rowan replied disappointed. She chimed in with her own toast. "To my sister and my soon to be brother. I wish you happiness and love forever, but don't forget she's my twin and I can come to raid your fridge any time I want." The room filled with laughter.

"In all seriousness, I'm so excited to marry this man. And since you are all here..." Halyn paused looking at Becca, Halyn, and Rowan all huddled on the couch. " I'd love for the three of you to be my bridesmaids and Rowan, would you do me the privilege of being my maid of honour?"

" I'd be insulted if you never asked, " Rowan replied as she finished off her bubbling pink champagne.

" I'd love to be such an important part of your wedding." Said, Becca.

" Let's plan a wedding!" Lucy shouted

Halyn awoke the next morning in her childhood bedroom, wrapped in the arms of her new fiancée, a term she felt would need getting used to. She had never been fond of the word. She turned over to face Tarek who was already awake, his bare chest was wavering up and down and his hair was flattened against his forehead. Not waking up beside him every day was unimaginable.

" Good morning fiancée. " He said as he turned towards her, lifting her hair from in front of her tired eyes.

"Good morning." She replied softly while simultaneously yawning.

" Are your worries about me sleeping with you in your childhood bedroom a thing of the past now?"

" Yes. Its just weird you know, I was never allowed to have boys in my room. But I had the best sleep I've had in months. It was such a perfect day yesterday and my brain was thankful for that."

" Well, I'm glad. I'm so happy for you, for us."

" Me too."

" I better make my way back to my apartment and continue packing. Would you like to come by to help me tonight?" He asked as he delicately kissed her shoulder.

" I promised the girls we would go out to celebrate tonight. How about tomorrow instead? I can bring breakfast and lattes and we can hang out in our jogging pants all day."

" Sounds like a perfect day, minus the packing part."

" Yes but you are packing to come and live with me remember?"

" You're right. There is nothing else I would rather be doing. I love you so much Halyn. I meant every word I said last night and everything I have said to you over the last three years. I don't know where I would be without you."

Halyn kissed Tarek and then pushed him off the bed playfully. " I love you too, now get up, or we will end up staying here all day."

" That's not the worst idea," Tarek shouted from the floor.

Halyn changed into a pair of jeans and a tank top. She wrapped her hair in a high top-knot. Makeup free, she made her way to the kitchen, embracing the aroma of freshly brewed coffee.

Rowan was sitting at the table, in a deep conversation on her phone. Halyn immediately knew it was a new love interest. Rowan didn't have actual phone conversations with just anyone, especially accompanied by the high pitched, giddy laugh she was projecting every few seconds. "This one might be a keeper." She thought to herself as she poured a large cup of coffee. Making her way to the table, Halyn sat beside her sister, mocking her flirtatious hair twirl.

"You know he can't see you doing that right now right?" she whispered.

Rowan was annoyed. " I'll call you back Ben when I have a bit more privacy. My sister just walked in."

Raising her eyebrows, Halyn asked, " Who's Ben?"

"A new interest."

"Love interest?"

" I don't know I've known him for like two weeks."

"Well, it seems like he's more than just a bit of an interest."

"Let's change the subject. Where do you want to go out tonight to celebrate? We could do the spa or the club."

" Is it my bachelorette party already? And those are two very different venues with polarizing vibes. Why don't we just go out for dinner? Perhaps somewhere casual?"

"Come on Halyn, you always do casual. This is an

exciting time for you, and it's our treat."

" OK, well how about the new wood fire pizza place close to Dryden? Will we make it back in time? I've heard great things about it."

"That's a great idea actually and I will make sure we are back in time. Fingers crossed they have a spot open tonight, I'm sure it books up fast. I'll call as soon as they open." Rowan said. " I'm really happy for you sis."

" Thanks, Rowan. We are very happy. And I'm still trying to absorb all of the extreme life changes that were thrown at me in the last twenty-four hours. I'm going to go out and sit in the hammock with my coffee."

"Ok good luck getting in it without spilling that hot coffee all over you."

" Challenge accepted," Halyn replied with confidence as she donned her flip flops and opened the patio door.

With her bare feet grazing the grass, Halyn made her way through the freshly manicured back yard to her sanctuary. It was a beautiful humid, sunny day. She was so grateful for yesterday and all it encompassed. She carefully and slowly sat into the precariously hung hammock, only spilling one drop of coffee onto the ground, saving both her clothing and the beverage itself. She looked over to the house, signalling a thumbs-up to her sister. Just as she put her coffee into her lap and settled into the hammock, a flood of anxiety filled her chest. In the distance, she could see her grandfather's guitar hanging in the garage, bringing her back to the day she sat with Zach in his room a few years ago. And although their relationship had fizzled away, she had maintained a respectable level of civility with him over the last year. She always kept a respectable distance from him. He still had feelings for her, and she was aware of it. It was painstakingly obvious at times and now she sat motionless and numb with an engagement ring on her finger, looking up at her granddad's guitar.

Worst of all, Zach was still dating Marissa, and Halyn knew that nothing would make Marissa happier than hearing about Halyn's recent personal events. No longer did Marissa have to worry about her submissive being linked to his ex and Halyn hated the idea of giving her exactly what she wanted. But, she knew they would find out soon enough and caring about what Marissa thought was not the priority, or at least it shouldn't be. She decided to shift focus to her upcoming celebration. For once, Halyn was more than excited for a night out on the town. After all, she was proud of herself for what she had accomplished and she was ticking off most of her life goal boxes.

CHAPTER 16

"Pizzaz", the new woodfire pizza joint was ablaze as the girls strolled in. Rowan, leading the group like she owned the place, was directing the hostess to the large round table at the back that was reserved for them, a private area of sorts, which Halyn appreciated. They were greeted and escorted back to the table that they, fortunately, reserved off of a last-minute cancellation that day. Rowan wasted no time before she ordered a full round of shots.

" Well, this night is going south really fast at this rate Rowan," Halyn stated half-jokingly.

" Stop being so negative. It's not every day my sister gets into medical school and engaged in one day. We are making memories here."

" I'm with her," Lucy added, pointing to Rowan.

Halyn decided to shift from pointless banter to appreciation. "Thank you, girls. I can't think of anyone I would rather celebrate with. And now that we will be seeing each other less frequently, we will have to make it a point to plan more nights like these.

"Well, we have all the wedding planning and

parties. Also, I don't mind helping you study." Becca chimed in.

" Yes, you are now my working friends with potential careers. It must feel so good to be finished school. Any job prospects for you yet Becca? Halyn asked.

" Actually yes. I am helping to create a commercial for a new vegan food company for the local cable channel starting next week."

" Well then, am I not allowed to order anything with meat on this menu now?' Asked Rowan, keeping her eyes on the menu.

" I am." Added Lucy. " That is a great project, Becca! There's more to celebrate than we thought."

" Have the two of you mapped out your travel plans yet?" Halyn pointed to Lucy and Rowan who had decided to take a year off to travel. According to Rowan, they were going to travel to Europe or South America, with no real plans, which sent Halyn's Type–A personality into over-drive.

"Yes! PARRRRRRIIISSSS! Exclaimed Rowan in a terrible, exaggerated French accent.

" We both decided that Paris was at the top of our lists. So we will start there and see where the trains take us." Said Lucy excitedly.

" How exciting!" Said Becca

As the waitress arrived with their drinks, Halyn couldn't help but wonder how long they would be in Europe. She couldn't imagine planning a wedding without them, especially without her twin sister. "How long will you be away"? She asked, unable to resist posing the question.

" We were originally planning for 3 months. But now that there is a wedding to plan, it will depend on when you think you will get married."

" Yeah, when do you think you'll get hitched?" asked Becca

"We haven't talked about it yet."

" Not at all? Not even a little before he proposed?"

" You had no idea he was going to propose did you?" Asked Rowan

" No, I didn't. We talked about moving in together and that's about it. So we have a lot to talk about now."

" He loves you. I've never seen anyone look at you the way he does. I wouldn't settle for any less for you."

" Thanks for your approval Rowan," Halyn replied sarcastically.

" Well, you know, if he doesn't meet the twin sister stamp of approval, we kick him to the curb. Literally. I'd do that and you know it. Alright, ladies, raise your shots to Halyn, the new doctor wife, let's get this party started!"

Halyn shuttered as she swallowed the fiery liquid. "Why on earth do people pay money for this?" She thought to herself. With her throat burning and her eyes watering she caught a glimpse two familiar faces in the window. Soon, another two familiar male faces appeared in the front window of the restaurant. Rowan noticed Halyn's frightened stare and looked out the window herself.

" Oh no! Is that the wolf pack?" Rowan asked. All four girls stopped dead in their tracks as they realized Zach and his entourage were making their way into the restaurant.

"We need to stop them!" Lucy said in a panic.

Rowan fled from the table in a state of desperation to stop Zach and his friends from entering the building before they could ruin the celebration. "Stop!" Rowan put her hand in Zach's face. "You can't come in here!"

" Do you own this place?" asked Eric sarcastically. Rowan gave Eric a soul-piercing glare, which sent all five of them a few steps backward.

" We are celebrating tonight and you can't ruin it."

" So are we." Chimed in one of the wolf pack members.

"Wait, what are you celebrating? Asked Zach.

" Halyn's acceptance into medical school." Rowan paused. "And her engagement to Tarek."

Zach took a few steps awkwardly backward and turned around in the opposite direction with a slow cadence. He pushed through the wolf pack and down the street alone. His friends followed him and soon Rowan realized, she had just shattered Zach's heart into a million pieces. She stood there and watched the group turning the corner, into a dark alley, Eric placing his hand around Zach's shoulder.

" She deserves better than you," Rowan whispered under her breath, as she went back into the bustling restaurant.

CHAPTER 17

Zach was unable to collect his thoughts. He kept walking with no end in sight, with no idea that his friends were feverishly following him. The emotions were overwhelming and he was becoming them, instead of just feeling them. A dark weighted cloud was over his head, the metaphor feeling incredibly real at the moment. He took a deep breath. It still didn't help. He sat on the bench for a few seconds, then stood back up before Eric could sit down beside him. He was manic. After kicking the wall of the restaurant numerous times, Eric decided to take action.

"Let's take you back to my place."

" I can't go there. Halyn lives there. She's engaged, Eric."

" Yeah and he's a nerd." One of the wolf pack members chimed in.

"You're not helping Josh," Eric replied annoyed.

"Where else can you go? You were going to come and stay with me anyway. You can't go back to the lake house. Marissa will just kick you out."

" I'm supposed to be celebrating my breakup with Marissa and my new chance with Halyn. Instead, I'm homeless and the love of my life is marrying someone else instead of me."

" Look, I can see you are crushed. You need to stay with me. Halyn lives at the other end of the hall. I barely ever run into her. The chances are really low and we can keep you incognito until you pull yourself together."

Reluctantly, Zach caved and went to Eric's apartment, with only two duffle bags in hand. Marissa had left him with nothing but his clothes and a toothbrush. When they arrived at Eric's place, Zach tossed his only bags beside the couch and sat motionless in one spot for hours contemplating his actions over the last three years.

"What was I thinking? What a waste of time. I'm such a fool."

" You aren't a fool. Well, maybe a little, but you also learned some very valuable lessons." Eric replied with self-proclaimed wisdom.

" Like never to be seduced by someone like Marissa Jacobs?"

" You were thinking with your little head more than your actual head like most 20-year-olds do. You're maturing now."

" That doesn't help now. She's engaged, Eric! I didn't see this coming at all."

"So where do we go from here? You can message her once you have diffused a little. Congratulate her and talk it out, which will probably leave you even more depressed, or you can just say nothing and come to the harsh realization that she has moved on. There are plenty of other fish in the sea."

" Yes but she's a mermaid in a sea of guppies. I can't see a life without her."

" That's the cheesiest thing I have ever heard you say. I think I need to keep a closer eye on you than I thought. Now you are talking crazy talk."

Zach let out a small laugh from the corner of his mouth. But he meant it. He couldn't see himself with anyone other than Halyn. " I've just put so much energy into finally getting Marissa to understand that we are no longer together, all in hopes of spilling my feelings to Halyn as early as tomorrow. Why couldn't I have done it sooner?"

" That's the ultimate question. You snooze you lose buddy." Eric replied, his brutal honesty in full force. " It wouldn't hurt for you to let her know how you are feeling though. At the very least, you owe her some kind of conversation after years of silence. It will at the very least flatter her and give you both some needed closure. Remember, she's been holding on to your breakup, or lack thereof for a while.

Zach soon realized that his distance and lack of attention to Halyn was his most colossal mistake. Maybe if he had simply talked to her, and maintained some kind of connection over the last three years, they would be in a different place now. But Marissa wouldn't allow it. She barely let him talk to a female cashier at a store, let alone his ex-girlfriend. He had wasted so much time on pleasing Marissa, that he had lost himself, and the love of his life in the process.

" I need to come up with a plan." He said spontaneously, as he stood up from the couch with rapid force.

"Ok, now you are scaring me," Eric answered. A plan for what exactly?"

" I need to reach out to her, and then take her somewhere special, somewhere that meant a lot to both of us when we were dating."

" And just where would that be?"

Zach pondered Eric's question for a few minutes as he paced the floor of the living room until he stopped in his tracks at the door of Eric's apartment. "I've got it." He put on his sneakers and his jacket as quickly as he could and stormed out of the apartment without saying goodbye to his friend.

" Text me please," Eric said shockingly. " Ok bye then." He shook his head and smiled at the thought of his friend who was chasing after a girl who was engaged.

Zach Payne raced to his car, almost falling on the gravel at the base of the curb where it was parked. He started the ignition and reversed his car, the tires screeching behind him. He had an idea that would surely convince Halyn to at the very least, sit down and talk to him. After driving erratically to the Central Hub, he went up to the library and fetched a few pieces of paper and a pen from the copying station, before returning down to the main hall. He scanned the room.

" Now for a quiet place where I can think." He thought to himself. But instead, he had a better idea. " Halyn's study nook!" He ran back upstairs into the library, exasperated. The few patrons who remained in the wee hours of the morning were caught off guard by Zach's panic and stared at him until he passed by. He found the fireplace at the center of the library and followed it up to the floor where Halyn studied almost every day. Sometimes Zach would pass through the library, just to catch a glimpse of her. " This is the best place for inspiration." He thought to himself. Sleep evaded him that night. He spent hours in the library on coffee and energy drinks, writing, over and over again, until he got exactly what he wanted on paper. And when the library closed, he took a break to go to the gym and then settled in the main hall of the Central Hub and continued to write until it was finished, until the song he wrote for Halyn, was perfect.

The sun was already up when Zach decided that a few hours of sleep would likely do him some good, just in case Halyn agreed to meet him later that same day. He was in rough shape, but feeling proud of what he had accomplished. He was ready to put his heart on his sleeve, knowing rejection may be around the corner. But what more did he have to lose? Making his way back to Eric's apartment, he fully mapped out his plan in his head. Of course, it meant Halyn agreeing to meet with him if not, his sleepless night was all for nothing. As he approached Guildwood, he decided that for the first time, he did not want to run into Halyn, so instead of going through the front entrance, he chose to go through the side door, which led straight to Eric's side of the hallway. Zach snuck in without knocking. "

"Eric!" he called.

Silence. He was still asleep. "Perfect." Zach thought as he made his way to the spare bedroom, where he dreamed of her for several hours.

Zach awoke from his dream reluctantly and looked at the clock. He was shocked to see it read 3:00 PM. He sat at the side of the bed until the light-headedness of day sleep wore off, perking up at the thought of Halyn. He picked up his phone, staring at it for a moment, with just a slight hesitation. He punched in her name on the smooth buttons of his old phone, took a deep breath in, and sent her a message.

"Hey, How are you? Long time no talk. Any chance we can meet up tomorrow? I've owed you an important chat for a while."

On the other side of the conversation, Halyn sat astonished at the message she had just received. "Now that I'm engaged he wants to talk? Isn't that like totally backward?" She asked out loud to Rowan, who was sitting beside her at the café as they sipped on lattes. Rowan was eyeing up the barista again. "Hello. Did you hear me?" Halyn asked annoyed at her sister's lack of attention in such an imperative moment.

"Don't answer it." Rowan bluntly replied.

"Why not?"

"Because I saw how much his heart broke when I told him you were engaged. Rowan's attention then turned towards her sister. "I'm not sure it's the best idea. You wouldn't want to give in to his games. He's put you through enough already."

"Maybe so, but I also know how it feels to have someone you love not answer, or give you the time of day," Halyn replied, with the memory flooding her mind. She moved it out of her consciousness before sadness could set it.

"On the flip side, maybe this way he can have a taste of his own medicine. String him along. Show him how it feels. And then have him apologize. You are engaged. There is nothing good that will come out of your meeting with him."

"But I've wanted this conversation for years. Maybe I will get some closure."

Halyn's justification was weak in Rowan's eyes. "Maybe you shouldn't marry someone else if you still need closure."

Rowan's words were like a sharp knife into Halyn's chest. But her words were accurate. She didn't owe Zach anything, but still, it wasn't in her genetics to just leave someone she cared for hanging. So without Rowan's approval or knowledge, she texted him back, not wanting to sound too enthusiastic."

"Sure. Where?"

CHAPTER 18

As Halyn made her way across the campus towards the building where her first-year classes were held, a wave of nostalgia hit her. She had woken up on little sleep, apprehensive for what the rest of the day would bring. She walked along the cobblestone pathways approaching the building where she first met Zach, Eric, Lucy, and Becca. Her first year of college was memorable and she was attempting to positively reflect on the last few years, knowing that one day, she would look back on them as some of the best years of her life.

The lengthy landscaped walkway led to a quaint new square that had just been built on the grounds of campus. She stopped at the calming fountain in the middle of the otherwise barren space. The serenity was exactly what she needed at the moment. The trickling water was continuously flowing through a pool of naturally parallel waves, similar to a fountain you would see in Rome. After a brief pause, she continued to make her way to the meeting point Zach had requested. She was to meet him at the intersection of Main and Park St. Although she had been at Dryden for four years, she never really paid much attention to the street names, since all students used buildings as landmarks instead. She looked down at her phone, studying her GPS until she came to the intersection. She waited briefly and studied the perimeter, no one else was there, including Zach. It was a Sunday and school was out for the year, so the campus was devoid of people.

"Why would he want to meet me here?" She thought to herself. And then suddenly, she remembered. Her first encounter with Zach came flooding back. And although it wasn't the most pleasant way to meet someone, never the less, it was the spot where they met. It was the very spot where she had narrowly evaded Zach's car. As she was re-hashing the experience in her mind, Zach appeared behind her. Without seeing him, she could hear his slow footsteps approaching, and could feel his eerie presence. She turned around slowly, meeting his longing gaze. His eyes were just as crystal clear as she remembered. He was dressed casually and appeared as though he hadn't slept for days, but what stood out the most, was that his guitar hung nimbly along his right shoulder.

"Hi." He said nervously.

" Hi Zach." Halyn chose to reply confidently, trying to maintain composure, knowing that assurance was key in the moment. " Are you playing somewhere later?" She pointed to his guitar.

"You could say that." A smile escaped Zach's uneasy expression, a little tension releasing from his shoulders. I thought we could go for a little walk. I think down memory lane is the saying."

" What do you mean?" she asked hesitantly, as she dissected his intentions.

"Just follow me."

" You're kind of scaring me a little." She replied, her assertiveness taking a dive.

" Trust me, you don't need to be afraid. When we are done, we can head to the café to talk. I owe you that much."

For some strange reason, Halyn's natural instinct was to trust him. After all, this is a man she adored at one point and he had helped shape the person she had become. Even though it meant many tears and sleepless nights, he had taught her a great deal about relationships, self-respect and what she didn't want in a relationship, although he may not have known it.

" Ok, but let's stay out in public, around campus."

" Well, we will stay out in public, but I can't promise on campus. Will you please trust me?"

Halyn could feel the sincerity in both his voice and his eyes, so she chose to trust him, remaining vigilant of her surroundings. " Okay fine, where are we going?"

"Lots of places. Think of it as a bit of a scavenger hunt. And this intersection, this very location is where I first laid eyes on you. " He smiled, pushing his guitar around his back, never taking his eyes off of her.

Curiosity filled Halyn's mind as she followed Zach back up the cobblestone walkway and into the building where they shared their first year classes. They walked inside the main doors, and into the dark, empty classroom. " This is where I first met you and realized I was attracted to you. Do you remember how mad you were that day?" They both let out a small laugh to break the ice.

" Yes. I wanted to run you over with your own car. Actually, I'm pretty sure Rowan was coming up with some sort of plan to do it herself."

"I believe it. She still terrifies me." They shared a laugh again.

" She scares me sometimes too and I share a genetic makeup with her."

Zach studied Halyn for a moment as she sauntered down to her old desk, relishing any minute he could get with her. He wished he had paid more attention when he had the time so many years ago. He still had no clue how this day would go, but if all went to plan, he was going to win her back with his charm. He allowed her to take her time, knowing she was appreciating more than just their time together. As she made her way back up the stairs, he caught a glimpse of the diamond on her left hand. Diverting his attention away from it, he opened the door to the classroom directing her out of the room. " Ladies first."

Catching up to her brisk pace, he stopped Halyn and guided her to the side door of the building. "This way." He reached for her hand, she pulled it away, pretending to tie her hair, although it was already neatly placed in a slicked-back ponytail. He had noticed it already. He loved how natural she looked. With his heart feeling a slight bit of disappointment, he led her towards the Central Hub.

After a minute of awkward silence, Zach remembered the one bit of news he was elated to hear. "Congratulations on getting into medical school. I heard. I always knew you could do it."

"You did? Funny you never said anything until now." Halyn was playing hardball. She was not going to let this be easy for him.

Zach was aware Halyn would be apprehensive in his quest but didn't know she would lay the guilt trip on him, although she had every right to be upset and confused. "I'm sorry about that." He replied apathetically.

Halyn glanced at him from the corner of her eye, making sure he didn't notice. She felt some guilt when she read his bleak expression. "Where to next?" she asked genuinely curious to see where the scavenger hunt would take them.

Just to the left of the Hub was the Grand Hall. Halyn had only been to a few events at the hall since she had come to Dryden. She was curious as to why they would stop there since she had spent such little time in the building. It wasn't long before she realized that Zach was taking her, not only to different locations in which they had been together, but was also taking her on a sort of timeline throughout their relationship. The hall is where they shared their first awkward encounter during the first year fling.

" This is where we first talked?" She asked. " I remember now, the First Year Fling was here."

" Precisely. But that's not why I remember it. This is where I first knew I had strong feelings for you. I wanted to ask you out so badly. Instead, I spilled a cupcake all over you. Best and worst day ever."

Halyn laughed nervously, tension rising in her face. She could feel a headache coming on. "I think I need to sit down for a minute."

She was no fool, catching on to Zach's intricate scheme. He was trying to win her back, and she needed to sit and think about how she was going to navigate the rest of this day. " What about Marissa?" She thought. She walked towards the far end of the hall as Zach remained at the front entrance. She sat on the window ledge that looked out onto the Hub, panic rising further in her chest. " Stay calm. This is what you wanted." It was true that she had fallen in love with another man, but she also needed closure and came to the conclusion, that regardless of what the day held, she needed to have that dire conversation with Zach before the day was out for her own mental well-being. So, she decided to continue with his plan, treading cautiously.

As she walked back towards Zach, she caught a glimpse of his innocent posture, which made it hard for her to keep her guard up, not to mention, he was still carrying his guitar around his neck and it had to be getting uncomfortable. " Do you want me to carry that for a minute?" She pointed to his guitar.

" This? Oh, that's kind of you, but I'll have a break with where we are going next."

" Okay, where to next?"

" Well, neither of us are going to like where we are going, but it needs to be done. Let's go."

Zach hastily led Halyn out of the grand hall, to the parking lot next to the Central Hub, a few spots away was Zach's car. She noticed it had been recently repaired and re-painted, not to mention, his engineering skills had greatly improved.

" You've done some impressive improvements on the car since I last saw it." She said, keeping the compliments to a minimum.

" Thank you. I'll take it." He replied as he opened the door for her. She climbed in gracefully. Zach was noting every delicate movement she made. It was almost as if he had developed a sixth sense for her. He admired the way she sat calmly on the passenger side. He took a deep breath in, relishing the moment with her, before driving off along the highway, a drive he had regrettably completed far too many times over the last three years.

Halyn's heart sank at the sight of Marissa's driveway. A large part of her knew that Zach's well thought out tour would inevitably take them to the lake house. Zach pulled over to the side of the road, making sure his car was out of Marissa's vision. He stepped out of the car and went over to Halyn's side, opening the door discreetly. "' Come with me he said, as he made his way to the trunk. Halyn sat still in the car. " Are you crazy?" She whispered loudly. "I don't want to go in there."

"We aren't."

"Well, it sure looks like it."

"Don't worry, I have unfortunately spent enough time here to know how we can remain out of sight. Just follow me and be quiet."

" Don't you live here?"

"Not anymore." He replied as he threw a wool blanket over his shoulder and placed his guitar in the trunk."

Surprised, she realized that Zach and Marissa were no longer an item. Halyn listened to Zach's request and followed him through a narrow, wooded path down to the lake. It was lined with thick trees and bushes maintaining a dense sheath of privacy away from the lake house. The lake house was a healthy distance away, so much so that Halyn felt that they were far enough, that they could walk and talk without hesitation.

" Just wait here a minute," Zach said as he

dashed around the bush onto the beach and out of sight. Halyn peaked through the bushes to get a glimpse of what he was up to, attempting to move branches out of her line of vision. Zach appeared suddenly behind her and her alarmed reaction caused him to startle as well. He regained his composure before continuing of the beaten path. " I have a little something for you."

They turned the corner and around the bushes, where in the distance, Halyn saw a soft, fur blanket around the bend of the beach. It was perched delicately on the rock in which they had spent their first night together at Marissa's lake house party. The memories of that night began to flood her consciousness as she walked beside Zach towards the blanket. She was hesitant to follow him further.

"Zach, I'm not so sure this is a good idea. Fist of all its trespassing, and secondly, this is not what I had in mind when we discussed being in public today."

" I'm not going to hurt you. I just want to talk. It will only be a few minutes. I promise we are almost done."

" I'm still with Tarek." She shouted, anxiety coursing through her veins.

" I know. Just trust me."

Pushing past Zach, Halyn made her way to the blanket on the rock. Zach reached out his hand to help her up the embankment but she declined his gesture. She sat down on the far corner of the blanket, making a statement that there was going to be a healthy distance between them. Zach read her intentions and he respected her body language as he sat on the other side of the blanket, leaning back onto his hands, studying her as she gazed out onto the lake.

" It's still just as beautiful as it was four years ago." She noted after a minute of complete and awkward silence.

"It is." Zach hesitated for a moment. "And so are you."

Halyn continued to look towards the lake, she didn't reply to his impulsive comment. She pondered what he might be up to, although she was pretty sure he had broken up with Marissa, she still wasn't sure if he would have the audacity to try and break her engagement off with Tarek.

"I wanted to bring you here because, well, this is where I truly fell for you. I knew I liked you a lot and...."

" Why are you doing this Zach? It's been four years, and now you are saying all of these endearing things when you could have addressed them on so many other occasions."

"I know Halyn, I was just confused."

" Just confused? So being confused is a good reason to just drop me like I never existed, and like all this, all these things we have been re-doing all day never happened? You broke me, Zach. No wait, you didn't just break my heart but I was also never worth an official break up, a conversation, or an apology. And that is what hurts the most. I applaud you and respect you for following your heart. That's what everyone should do. But how you did it, was downright selfish and not to mention spineless. You have no idea what I went through or how it changed me. I've had to rebuild my self-confidence and self-worth over the years and I feel as though right now, you are trying to tear them back down again. I wish you knew how much you destroyed me when you left."

" I wanted to talk to you Halyn. I just didn't know what to say. And then I was with Marissa and she was brainwashing me and....."

" Take some accountability for your own actions Zach. I have given you plenty of opportunities to discuss our relationship over the years, but you ignored every one of them. That is a choice you made. So why on earth, would you ever think I would ever want to be with someone who would disrespect me like that?"

Zach sat in silence, tears welling up in his eyes. This was not the response he was expecting. He knew Halyn may have some criticism lined up for him, but this was resentment and at the moment, he wished he could take it all away. But it was too late.

" Are you angry?" Halyn asked him, reading his

solemn expression that must have appeared like anger to her.

" No, I'm numb." He replied, and he had never been more truthful in his life. They sat in silence for another few moments before Halyn came to sit beside him. She could see he was crying, but trying to hold back his tears.

" Now is your chance to apologize or at least make me feel better about how you treated me. I wish we could have had a conversation three or four years ago, and I think if we would have, we both would be in a better place right now, with each other. But clearly, now is all we have, and we need to get it off our chests, for everyone's sake, just the two of us, and no one else has to know about it. "

He looked at her with more love than he ever did. Her heart melted as she grabbed his hand and held it tightly, as much as she resented Zach for what he did, she still cared about him and hated seeing him so hurt.

" I have one more place for us to go." He said.

" Really? Now?" She asked, frustrated that he wouldn't follow through.

" Yes, let's go back up to the car. I promise I will answer all of your questions and lay it all out on the line at our next stop."

"I need you to be honest Zach, and explain to me why you did what you did."

" I will." He replied, his voice still raspy.

Halyn reluctantly followed Zach as they made their way back to the car, and drove back down the highway, past the school and into the downtown core of the city. The streets were bustling with locals and tourists alike, soaking in the summer heat. The atmosphere was inviting and refreshing. The patios adjacent to each restaurant were packed with students, and families lined the waterfront sharing ice cream cones and feeding ducks. Halyn was looking forward to another summer of relaxation before medical school started although now, she also had a wedding to plan. Her mind shifted to Tarek and guilt rose in her chest as she sat beside Zach in his car, on some kind of scavenger hunt date with him. She had to remind herself that today's events had a purpose that would help her and Tarek in the long-run, so with that, she was at peace.

Zach pulled up to the parking lot beside the pier, and across from The Orr restaurant. She was curious as to why he would bring her here since they never been to the restaurant together. It was getting close to lunchtime though and she thought that maybe Zach was hungry. She certainly had no appetite with everything that was happening.

" You go ahead in and I will catch up to you in a minute." He instructed her.

" Go in where?" Halyn asked honestly

" The restaurant." I reserved a table. Just give

them my name. I will be right behind you."

" Okay." Halyn caught a glimpse of Zach heading for his trunk as she walked across the street towards the front of the restaurant. She hesitated when she read the sign on the front door. " CLOSED".

" That's strange." She said out loud. "He said he had a reservation." She knocked on the door as she saw a figure slide past the window. The door of the restaurant opened, and a friendly man greeted her, encouraging her to step inside.

" Come in madam." He said.

" Thank you." She entered the foyer of the restaurant sheepishly. "Please call me Halyn. Madam makes me feel old. I am here for a reservation under the name of Zach Payne? But I'm confused since the sign on the door says you are not open."

" My pleasure Halyn. Please, come this way."

"I'm sorry?" She asked, surprised that she was able to enter the building.

" We were expecting you."

" But the sign says you are closed."

" Not for you." The server replied with a devious look in his eyes. " Follow me. You are the guest of honour today."

The host led Halyn through the restaurant, which was empty. Halyn had never seen The Orr empty. It was the busiest restaurant in the city, and it was a fight to get a reservation on the slowest of days. So, seeing it uninhabited was perplexing. She walked past the exposed brick bar towards a set of stairs that was illuminated with burning candles. The path of candles led to a beautiful barn wood sliding door in the basement of the restaurant. Halyn was unaware that the space existed. She had only been on the main floor. In fact, she had never seen anyone go downstairs.

"After you Madam, I mean Halyn."

"You want me to go in there?" She pointed to the darkened room with the sliding barn door.

"Precisely."

" Is it a dungeon? Halyn asked half-joking and half-serious.

" No Miss. This is the Private dinner suite. Guests can enjoy a quiet private space for an extra fee. You are a very lucky lady, it is rarely available."

Halyn then realized that Zach must have been planning the day's events for some time if this private dinner suite was in such demand.

"Thank you.... I'm sorry, what's your name?"

"Henry Madam..... Halyn rather."

"Well thank you, Henry."

Halyn watched Henry as he made his way back up the stairs, admiring his pretentious posture. She turned towards the impeccable barn door, the detail in the carpentry was magnificent. She grasped the handle and slid the door open where it revealed a stone fireplace that was crackling in the distance. She stepped forward into the entranceway, where she saw Zach standing at the end of an elegant, solid wood table, his guitar around his neck, and a bouquet of Gerber daises in his hand.

She gasped for air. " Oh no!" Her expression diffused from shock to contempt, while his was euphoric and filled with so much hope. She quickly calmed herself, knowing that anger and resentment wouldn't get her anywhere in this scenario.

Just as she opened her mouth to speak, Zach began quietly playing a tune on his guitar, his gaze fixed on Halyn. In his right hand, strumming along the guitar strings delicately, was the guitar pick she had gifted him so many years ago. Tears welled up in Halyn's eyes as the volume and cadence of his song picked up. Feeling awkward, yet flattered, Halyn sat on the chair directly in front of her. She was feeling faint. She listened to him, absorbing the song that he had written just for her. It coursed through her veins like razor blades and each time she heard the chorus, her heart sank a bit further. She realized how much effort he had put into the song and the day's events.

But still, she was left uneasy. Something still didn't feel right. As he continued to sing, she stayed focused on his expression. It was honest, but not passionate, lovable but not sincere. She studied him more. The words were everything any girl would want to hear, but she still didn't feel the flood of love she thought she should. It was then that she realized that his actions never met his words. He had still never apologized or owned up for what he did to her. He had never reached out to her in all the time that they were at Dryden, and if he really wanted to be with her, he would have made the effort then. His feelings although he likely thought they may be, were not genuine. He was not her person.

As he finished the last note of his song on the guitar, Halyn analyzed her thoughts, trying to come up with a suitable reaction in a split second, attempting to be a realist, but also respectful. She gave him a gentle applause. " Thank you for that. It was lovely."

Zach came down and sat beside her. " What do you think? Will you take me back Halyn? I think we are meant to be together."

Exasperated, Halyn sighed heavily. " You see, that's precisely the problem Zach. You THINK we are meant to be together. I need someone who is SURE and who has never doubted it, someone who has always wanted to scream it from the rooftops that they love me. I want....... No, I need someone who is never insecure about our relationship, someone who values the person they are with."

" I value you more than anyone right now."

"You think you do, and I don't just want someone who values me right now. "

" What do you mean? You don't know what I am

thinking. I don't care how complicated it is, I just want to be with you."

" No, you are right. I don't know exactly what you are thinking. But I do know, that your actions don't match your words, and that's not entirely your fault. You like the idea of us. You like the idea of being with someone better than Marissa and I am comfortable for you." She paused a moment as she could feel the tension in Zach's posture as he moved farther away from her and removed his guitar from around his neck. " Zach, when you undoubtedly love someone, when that person is truly meant for you, you would do anything to be with them. You don't ghost them, and then wait four years to profess your love, and most certainly, at the very least, you apologize for your mistakes. You never did any of that for me until now, and I'm sorry, but it's too little too late. When you find the right person, nothing would stop you from all of these things. I'm not sure I could fully trust you or feel secure in a relationship with you again, and relationships are built on trust. I'm so sorry Zach, but I'm marrying Tarek."

Just then, Henry appeared with two intricate silver platters in each hand, exquisite red napkins were draped over his forearms. His welcoming smile turned to an awkward stare when he picked up on the vibe of the conversation in front of him.

" I'm sorry Henry. We are not hungry at the moment. I will come up and pay the bill for the room." Zach said solemnly.

"Very well sir," Henry replied as he made his way back through the barn door and up the candlelit path.

Halyn and Zach followed him up the stairs in awkward silence. And although the mood was somber, Halyn felt as though a weight had been lifted off of her shoulders. Although she never heard the apology she had hoped for, she had reached the closure she needed. As Zach met with Henry at the bar, Halyn made her way outside of The Orr and paused for a moment trying to figure out the best way to get back to Guildwood. She walked partway past the restaurant until she heard Zach's voice call for her again. He yelled from a distance.

" And this is the place I realized I made the worst mistake of my life, and that I realized I loved you, that night when I saw you with him for the first time."

Halyn paused and closed her eyes while taking a deep breath before turning towards Zach for one last time. She walked over to him and hugged him gently.

" I'm sorry Halyn. I never meant to hurt you, and I honestly can't imagine my life without you." He said desperately as he pulled her in tighter. She pulled herself away briskly knowing the hug meant something completely different to him. When she had almost fully let go, he clutched her hand, leaving something in it. She looked down to see her Grand-dad's guitar pick in the palm of her hand.

" I'm sorry too. I loved you too, but I never loved you enough to be ok with being your second choice.

"You were never my second choice. It's always been you Halyn."

She released Zach's hand and walked away, around the corner until Zach could no longer see her. Empowerment overcame her at that moment, for she felt as though she had found herself again. Never again would she allow a man to manipulate his way to her heart or play with it like a metaphorical yo-yo. Lessons had been learned, and some of them she would carry with her throughout her life. Not all she had experienced with Zach was amiss, but she now knew what she no longer had to tolerate. Through the heartbreak and revival of self-discovery, she learned what true, raw love should feel like, and she would never settle for anything less again. She would never be anyone's second choice. She clinched the guitar pick in her hands as she made her way back home to Tarek, the one who loved her without a doubt.

Acknowledgements

I would first like to thank my family for allowing me to put the time and energy required into this first novel. In particular, I am grateful to my daughters for inspiring me to write a story about empowerment and love combined, in hopes that it may guide them, their peers and the younger generations along their own journey someday.

A huge shout out to my stellar and dedicated launch team, Olga Bougie, Stephanie Brown, Brenda Dainton, Michaela Doolittle, Devon Dunning, Diana Figueiredo, Nicole Filion, Mandy Fletcher, Laurie Gedcke-Kerr, Melanie Knapp, Randi Kyle, Sarah Lewis,
J. McCarthy, Courtney Parry, Heather Paul, Marie Rogers, Marsha Snyder, Tennielle Suckow, Samantha Taylor, Amanda Trottier, Melissa Tsuji, Brittany VandenTillaart, Vicki Wellbanks and Lauren Whiteside-Scott. I cannot thank you all enough for the support.

To Jay Brown, who six years ago, inspired me to " Just keep writing. No matter how hard it gets." It truly kept me going. To Aileen Lavin for editing my initial draft and critiquing my work with such elegance. To my sister Lindsay Dainton for helping me with all the technical conundrums. And last but not least, to my editing team, Dave and Maureen, I would not have had enough confidence to publish without you.

Cover Photo By: Shuttershock

Manufactured by Amazon.ca
Bolton, ON